"Can You Take What We Have Now And Not Think About The Future?"

Cal asked.

Lara didn't hesitate. "Yes. After waiting so long for you, yes."

"It's the only way to make sure my trouble doesn't ruin your life, too. I've been selfish enough to get involved with you when I knew I shouldn't. I should have run in the other direction the day we met, but you were too tempting."

"I don't understand."

"Don't ask me any questions and you won't force me to lie to you," he said flatly.

"All right. But promise me you won't stop this time."

"I can't stop," he muttered as he pushed her loose top off her shoulders and sought her satiny skin with his mouth. "Not anymore."

Dear Reader,

This month: strong and sexy heroes!

First, the Tallchiefs—that intriguing, legendary family—are back, and this time it's Birk Tallchief who meets his match in Cait London's MAN OF THE MONTH, *The Groom Candidate.* Birk's been pining for Lacey MacCandliss for years, but once he gets her, there's nothing but trouble of the most *romantic* kind. Don't miss this delightful story from one of Desire's most beloved writers.

Next, nobody creates a strong, sexy hero quite like Sara Orwig, and in her latest, *Babes in Arms,* she brings us Colin Whitefeather, a tough and tender man you'll never forget. And in Judith McWilliams's *Another Man's Baby* we meet Philip Lysander, a Greek tycoon who will do anything to save his family...even pretend to be a child's father.

Peggy Moreland's delightful miniseries, TROUBLE IN TEXAS, continues with *Lone Star Kind of Man.* The man in question is rugged rogue cowboy Cody Fipes. In *Big Sky Drifter,* by Doreen Owens Malek, a wild Wyoming man named Cal Winston tames a lonely woman. And in Cathie Linz's *Husband Needed,* bachelor Jack Elliott surprises himself when he offers to trade his single days for married nights.

In Silhouette Desire you'll always find the most irresistible men around! So enjoy!

Lucia Macro

Senior Editor

Please address questions and book requests to:
Silhouette Reader Service
U.S.: 3010 Walden Ave., P.O. Box 1325, Buffalo, NY 14269
Canadian: P.O. Box 609, Fort Erie, Ont. L2A 5X3

DOREEN OWENS MALEK

BIG SKY DRIFTER

SILHOUETTE Desire®
Published by Silhouette Books
America's Publisher of Contemporary Romance

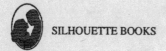

SILHOUETTE BOOKS

ISBN 0-373-76097-3

BIG SKY DRIFTER

This edition published by arrangement with Harlequin Books S.A.

Printed in U.S.A.

Books by Doreen Owens Malek

Silhouette Desire

Native Season #86
Reckless Moon #222
Winter Meeting #240
Desperado #260
Firestorm #290
Bright River #343
Roughneck #450
Arrow in the Snow #747
The Harder They Fall #778
Above the Law #869
Daddy's Choice #983
Big Sky Drifter #1097

Silhouette Romance

The Crystal Unicorn #363

Silhouette Intimate Moments

The Eden Tree #88
Devil's Deception #105
Montega's Mistress #169
Danger Zone #204
A Marriage of Convenience #282

Silhouette Special Edition

A Ruling Passion #154

DOREEN OWENS MALEK

is a former attorney who decided on her current career when she sold her fledgling novel to the first editor who read it. Since then, she has gained recognition for her writing, winning honors from *Romantic Times* magazine and the coveted Golden Medallion Award from the Romance Writers of America. She has traveled extensively throughout Europe, but it was in her home state of New Jersey that she met and married her college sweetheart. They now live in Pennsylvania.

One

Lara Daniels pulled into the service station and left her car at the pump, unfastening her seat belt and sliding out the passenger door. She straightened slowly, easing the cramp in her lower back; she had been driving for five hours nonstop and felt like a pretzel. The sky spread above her, a cloudless azure, dominated by an incandescent sun. It beat down on the road she had just left and created a shimmering mirage dancing on the distant asphalt.

"Hot, huh?" the attendant said, coming up behind her.

Lara nodded.

"And it's only June," he added, grinning, wiping his forehead with a greasy rag he had produced from the pocket of his stained jeans.

"Could you fill the tank for me?" Lara asked,

calling over her shoulder as she walked toward the convenience store at the back of the lot.

"Sure thing," the boy responded. "Cash or charge?"

"Cash," Lara said, pushing open the glass door of the store, sighing as a frigid blast of air conditioning hit her like a soothing wave. She went to one of the cases along the back wall and selected a can of juice, holding the freshly sweating container against her flushed face as she fished in her purse for change.

"No AC in your car?" asked the clerk sympathetically.

"It quit around Bozeman and I didn't have time to stop and get it fixed," Lara replied, handing the woman the coins.

"Traveling?"

"Yes. I drove out from the Chicago area to spend the summer with my grandmother. She has a horse ranch near Red Springs."

"It's going to be a scorcher," the clerk said, shaking her iron-gray-haired head. "When it's this bad before Independence Day you can bet we'll be topping a hundred soon. I've lived here all my life, and I know." She handed Lara a dime.

"Is the turnoff for Red Springs down that road?" Lara asked, pointing.

The woman nodded. "About eight miles. Do you have good local directions? It's pretty rural that way."

"Yes, I have everything written down, and I'm hoping I'll recognize some things. I used to come here with my parents when I was younger, but I haven't been back in about eleven years."

"It hasn't changed much. The horse breeders are a stubborn lot, they won't sell off to the resort developers, and we're way too far from any big cities for commuters, so we don't attract them. It's pretty quiet out here."

"That sounds good to me," Lara said, and meant it. After spending ten months chasing thirty noisy five-year-olds around an Illinois elementary school, she was looking forward to open skies, rosy sunsets and golden silence.

"Have you got a phone I could use?" Lara asked the clerk. "I'd like to check in with my grandmother. She knows I'm arriving today, but not what time."

"Sorry. The pay phone's been out for about a week."

Lara shrugged. "I guess I'll just have to show up and surprise her, then."

"Good luck in finding your way there," the clerk called, as Lara left.

Lara waved to her in farewell, made a stop at the outside rest room and paid the attendant for her gas. By the time she was behind the wheel of her car again, she began to feel a slight twinge of excitement and nostalgia at seeing her grandmother Rose's home once more.

Lara was an only child and both of her parents had died. Rose was her father's mother, and since the sudden loss of her youngest son Ron last winter to leukemia, Rose had been trying to run the thirty-acre spread with just the help of several hands. When

Rose suffered a slight stroke in late May, Lara canceled her plans to spend the summer as a camp counselor in the Adirondacks and decided to come to Montana instead. Rose had protested, but Lara had insisted, starting the drive to Red Springs just two days after the school year ended. And now she was almost there, about to see the stud farm for the first time since she was sixteen.

The flat, rolling grasslands slipped by her window as she drove toward Red Springs, thinking about the tasks that lay before her. Rose said that the hired men were handling the horses, but Lara knew that there was a lot of bookkeeping involved in her grandmother's business. Uncle Ron had done it until he died, and now Rose's failing health was preventing her from keeping up with it, although she was too stubborn to admit that and refused to turn the job over to an accountant permanently. Lara planned to whip the books into shape and then see what else could be done to help her grandmother before she returned to her teaching job in the fall.

She glanced down at the sheet of memo paper in her hand, turning at a signpost onto a smaller side road paved with loose stones. She had a vague memory of the dairy farm on the left, where cows and sheep roamed desultorily in the heat, cropping the browning grass, but it had been so long since her last visit that she wasn't really sure of anything. Lara's father had had some tiff with his brother Ron when she was in high school, and ever after Tom Daniels had insisted his mother come to see him in Chicago, where he wouldn't have to encounter Ron. Tom had never returned to the ranch and neither had his daughter, until this day.

Lara spotted the weatherbeaten sign reading "El Cielo" and turned onto the dirt track, examining with interest the new paddocks and practice rings that led away into the distance on either side of the road. She could see the ranch house at the top of a small rise, its stucco exterior recently whitewashed, its back veranda cooled by the shade of the grove of trees that surrounded it.

Several of the workers looked up from their tasks as Lara bounced past in her compact car, her head almost hitting the roof every time she struck a rut. Lara was tall and willowy, with the type of figure that drove skinny teenagers to despair but turned them into fashion models a few years later. She had tied her honey blond hair back in a ponytail, and with her face clean of makeup and her lean body clad in a tailored shirt and jeans, she looked like an ingenue in a fifties film. But she was not concerned with the impression she made as she parked her car in the paved circle in front of the house and bounded up the redbrick steps. She was so eager to see her grandmother that she tapped on the screen door and rang the bell at the same time.

Lara waited, listening as footsteps advanced down the hall from the kitchen. Two large pots of impatiens spilled their scarlet blooms on either side of the small front landing, and she was just bending to touch one of the velvet blossoms when the door opened.

Lara straightened and flung her arms around her

grandmother's narrow shoulders. "Rose! Oh, I'm so happy to see you."

She hugged the old lady, whom she had called by her first name since her toddler years. Rose felt thin in her arms, frail and birdlike. Lara held Rose off to look at her.

Rose's eyes were filled with tears; she was too overcome to speak, but she smiled tremulously, touching Lara's cheek.

Lara was shocked at Rose's appearance, though she tried not to show it. Once she took in her grandmother's bony face, shaking hands and weary expression, Lara knew that her decision to spend the summer in Montana had been the right one.

If anyone looked in need of some rest and a helping hand, it was Rose Daniels.

"Come inside, dear, and have a cool drink," Rose finally said, finding her voice. "You've had such a long trip."

Even Rose's voice was different, her delivery more hesitant than Lara remembered. For the first time, Rose's walk and manner showed her seventy-eight years. A whole team of doctors had assured Lara over the phone that her grandmother's stroke had been serious but not life-threatening, but looking at Rose now, Lara wasn't so sure.

"Are you feeling all right, Anma?" Lara asked, her concern causing her to revert to her baby nickname for Rose.

"Fit as a fiddle, especially now that you're here," Rose said, leading her down the red-tiled hall to the sunny kitchen, which had been opened up to include a breakfast nook since Lara had last seen it. But in general the whole place seemed much smaller than Lara recalled, maybe just because she herself was bigger; the house had expanded exponentially in her memory.

"I'll get you some lemonade," Rose said, heading for the refrigerator.

"Sit down, Rose, I'll get it," Lara interjected quickly. She was aware of her grandmother's grateful sigh as Rose sank onto one of the kitchen chairs. "Are the glasses still in this cabinet here?"

Rose nodded, and Lara got them both a drink, sitting across from Rose and handing her a tall tumbler filled with cloudy liquid and clinking ice.

"When did you last see your doctor?" Lara asked.

Rose closed her eyes, making a dismissive hand gesture Lara had seen her father use many times. "Please, not yet. No medical discussions just now—I am fed to the teeth with them. Let's talk about you. How was your trip? I really wish you had flown out here. It would have been so much more comfortable for you."

"I like to drive, and it was cheaper," Lara replied, not adding that she had wanted familiar transportation on hand in case of any emergency with her grandmother.

"So where did you stay last night?" Rose asked, clearly planning to divert the conversation into small talk. Lara allowed her to do it, since there was plenty of time for her to get an update on Rose's condition from her doctor. She had spoken to the cardiac specialist many times on the phone from Chicago and still had his number.

After giving Rose the details of her trip, they reminisced about Lara's childhood until Rose, who was clearly getting tired, said, "Can I get you some lunch, dear? It's almost time, and you must be famished after your long drive this morning."

"I'm not hungry, Rose. Why don't you lie down for a while and I'll get my things out of the car."

Rose nodded, clearly relieved that she didn't have to entertain Lara anymore. "I've prepared the new guest room for you. Your uncle Ron put on two new bedrooms at the same time he enlarged the kitchen. Of course, your father never saw the addition," she concluded sadly, her expression morose.

Lara took Rose's arm and led her to the back of the house. The hall had been extended by about fifteen feet and now opened up to a new master bedroom on the left and a smaller room with a bath on the right. Lara saw through the door that the guest room double bed was freshly made up and a vase of flowers stood on the bureau.

"There's chicken salad in the refrigerator if you change your mind about lunch," Rose said, still trying to feed her.

"Thanks," Lara said, guiding the older woman to the bed.

"Do you want me to call Cal to help you unload your car?" Rose mumbled, as Lara turned down the spread.

"Who's Cal?"

"Cal Winston, the hired man. I told you about him, Lara."

"You did not, Rose. I thought Jim Stampley was still your foreman."

"Jim is still with me, but he just oversees the business. Since Ron's illness, the house was falling apart, so I needed somebody to do odd jobs and run errands, that sort of thing. I hired Cal almost two months ago. I give him the loft above the stable, his meals and a small salary. He's been more than worth it, and it makes me feel secure to have a man around all the time."

Lara fluffed a pillow and Rose lay back immediately, closing her eyes. Lara took off her grandmother's shoes and then drew the coverlet over her, wondering if it had ever occurred to Rose that Cal himself might be a breach of security.

"He's living here on the place?" Lara asked slowly.

"The loft was empty and he needed a place to stay."

"How did you find him?" Lara asked, picturing a middle-aged road bum with a seamed face, few teeth and a drinking problem.

Her concern must have been obvious in her tone, because Rose's eyes shot open and she said defensively, "Cal has been a savior around here, Lara, you have no idea. In the past few weeks he has whitewashed the entire house, fixed the troughs in the stable and repaired the barn doors, not to mention run back and forth to town with the pickup for supplies and helped Jim with the horses. Today he's mending the fence in the south paddock. I don't know what I would do without Cal."

"How did you find him?" Lara asked again, more firmly, disregarding the monologue.

"I advertised in the Bozeman paper and he answered the ad," Rose replied, her voice fading.

"You hired a drifter who just showed up here?" Lara asked in a strong voice.

"He's not a drifter," Rose protested.

"Did he show you any references?"

"Really, Lara, I can't understand why you're making such a fuss. He's a fine young man, a hard worker. He's had some bad luck and he just needs some time in a quiet place to get his life together." Rose turned her head on the pillow to indicate that the conversation was over and closed her eyes again.

Lara didn't have the heart to grill her exhausted grandmother about Cal's nebulous "bad luck," but the picture forming in her mind unnerved her. All the workers came in by day and Rose was in an obviously vulnerable position, spending her nights alone in the house at the ranch; it would be easy for an opportunist to move in and take advantage of her.

Lara determined to find out about this Cal at her earliest opportunity.

She left Rose sleeping in the bedroom and went back to the kitchen, where she made herself a sandwich. She was actually starving, but had lied to her grandmother so Rose wouldn't insist on preparing the meal. She looked around the room as she chewed, noting the stack of prescriptions impaled by a spike on the polished counter. She would call Rose's doctor this afternoon, but first she would have a look at her grandmother's lodger. As she swallowed the last bite of bread she dusted her hands on her jeans and then left the house by the back door.

It was even hotter than it had been when she arrived. The noonday sun beat down on her as though it were a hammer as she left the yard by the gate and set off across the grass toward the south paddock. On the way she encountered a hand she didn't recognize and said, "Is Cal working down that way?"

He looked up and nodded mutely, then went back to stacking bales of hay.

Lara moved on, skirting a practice ring and catching sight of a figure at the far end of the fenced paddock. The man was kneeling, driving nails into a fresh redwood slat, facing away from her. As she came closer she realized that he was young and slim, no more than thirty, with jet black hair and the well-muscled back of an athlete. She hardly had time to absorb this shock before he heard her step behind him and glanced around at her.

"Cal?" she said, feeling foolish, as if she had been caught sneaking up on him.

He put down the hammer and stood, turning to face her.

"I'm Lara Daniels," she said. "Rose's granddaughter."

He nodded. "Rose told me you were coming to stay for a while. She's been looking forward to it."

They stared at each other in silence. Lara observed that he was tall, topping her by at least four inches, and lithe; his arms and abdomen were as well-defined as his back. His sweat-stained jeans were slung low on narrow hips, and a trickle of perspiration bisected his broad chest and ran under his belt. Lara raised her gaze quickly to his face; he was regarding her impassively, his heavily lashed dark brown eyes fixed on hers.

Lara stared. No words came to her mind.

"Do you need something, Miss Daniels?" he finally asked.

Lara cleared her throat. "Please, call me Lara. Rose said that your meals were included with the job. Did you want lunch?"

He took a handkerchief from his back pocket and wiped his face with it. "Rose just gives me dinner. I take something from the kitchen in the morning for the rest of the day."

"Oh, I must have misunderstood. Rose fell asleep before she could tell me the details."

"Is she okay?" Cal asked quickly, tossing the handkerchief on top of the T-shirt that lay discarded on the ground.

"I think so, but she's tired. I'm going to check in with her doctor later today."

He nodded. As he turned his head to glance back at his work, she noticed that his thin nose was slightly arched at the bridge, his lower lip fuller than his upper one, cushioning it. His chin was firm, with a slight cleft, giving his profile a chiseled, Roman cast. Lara felt herself staring again and then deliberately looked away.

"Is there anything else?" he asked pointedly, lounging back against the fence, one arm hooked over its top rail. He regarded her levelly, his damp hair curling onto his forehead and around his ears, giving him a boyish, tousled look.

"Uh, no, I guess not. You can get back to your job," Lara replied. She turned to walk away. When she glanced over her shoulder he was already gripping his hammer, holding the lower rail in place.

Lara rushed away as if afraid of what might happen if she stayed too long.

She was back in the kitchen, telephoning Rose's doctor, before she realized she had never asked the hired man for his references.

Rose woke at two and ate the hot lunch Lara had prepared. They spent the afternoon going over a portion of the business books and arguing about Lara's call to the doctor; he had recommended that Rose come in for a visit the next day and Rose steadfastly refused. By the time Lara added up the last column of figures to be checked on her portable calculator, it was five-thirty.

Rose got up from her chair to exclaim, "I'd better start dinner. Cal will be here at six, sharp."

"Isn't it a lot of work for you to cook for him every night?" Lara asked.

"Nonsense. What else do I have to do? It's a pleasure to feed a young man's hearty appetite, and I'd be drinking soup out of a can for supper if it weren't for him. It's no fun to make meals just for myself, and no fun to eat alone."

Lara silently conceded that point, but then said, "I want to talk to him concerning his background, Rose.

You really don't know anything about his past. I meant to ask him some questions earlier today but I forgot."

Rose turned from the stove and faced her granddaughter, her expression grim. "Lara Marie, I forbid it," she said firmly. "Cal's been working for me for two months and I've been more than satisfied. He doesn't have to prove himself to you all over again. I am paying him, and I'll be the judge of his suitability for his job. Now if I find out that you have been cross-examining him I will be very upset, do you understand me?"

"But, Rose—"

"You heard me, and that's final. You've been living in the city too long, my girl. You see a criminal behind every lamppost. Now help me with this meal. You can slice the mushrooms and the shallots while I bread the fish."

Lara got up and followed Rose's instructions, helping with the food and then setting the table. She was rinsing lemons in the sink when she looked through the window and saw Cal step up to the pump in the backyard. Her uncle Ron had installed it when he dug a new well during a long-ago dry spell.

Cal had a clean shirt and a towel folded over his arm; he set both items on the grass, then picked up a cake of brown soap sitting on the stone base of the well. He stripped off the T-shirt he had worn during the day and then cranked the pump handle, dousing his head and upper body with water. Lara watched as he lathered his face and torso and hands, then sluiced them liberally, finally grabbing the towel and drying off vigorously.

"He does that every night," Rose said at Lara's elbow, making her jump. "I look forward to seeing it all day."

Lara turned to look at her grandmother in astonishment; the old lady winked at her.

"He's made me put down my dishrag more than once," Rose added slyly.

Lara could feel herself blushing to the roots of her hair. She didn't know what to say.

"Don't be embarrassed," Rose said, walking past her to add the mushrooms to the pan. "I may be in my dotage but I still have an appreciation for the healthy male animal. And that one is a fine example of the species."

Lara made a great fuss of slicing the lemons she held, still not answering.

"Kind of makes me glad there's only a half bath in the loft," Rose went on kiddingly. "Ron was always talking about adding a shower, but he never quite got around to it."

"What will Cal do when winter comes?" Lara asked.

"I guess I'll just have to let him take a shower in the house," Rose said, and grinned broadly.

They heard footsteps on the back porch and then a knock on the screen door.

"Come on in, Cal," Rose called. "Dinner's almost ready."

The door opened and Cal entered the kitchen, instantly filling it with his masculine presence. Rose turned off the stove burner and lifted the filets onto a serving plate as Cal loomed in the background.

"Sit down, son," Rose said.

Lara put the bowls of rice and vegetables on the table, then added the pitcher of iced tea. The three of them sat and then Rose folded her gnarled hands on the table to say a prayer.

Lara glanced at Cal; he bowed his damp head respectfully, but did not pray.

Rose was full of questions about the repairs Cal was doing, and Lara said little as Cal described his work. He ate steadily and with enthusiasm, giving short and pithy answers in his resonant baritone, always deferring to Rose when speaking. His attitude was that of a favored, if roguish, student deferring to the local schoolmarm: "yes, ma'am" and "no, ma'am" were the rule of the day. It was clear that Rose was quite taken with him, treating him as if he were a member of the family. Certainly his looks would make any woman susceptible to his low-key charm, and he did appear able and industrious. But Lara had to wonder what someone of his seeming capabilities was doing mending fences for an hourly wage on a rural Montana ranch.

"Like it, Lara?" Rose asked.

Lara realized that her grandmother had been speaking to her. She looked from one face to the other, striving for a clue.

"I beg your pardon?" she finally said, nonplused.

"Don't you like the trout?" Rose asked. "You've hardly touched a bite."

"Oh, I'm sorry, I guess I'm not very hungry."

Lara took a large mouthful of the rice and chewed enthusiastically.

"Would you like something else?" Rose asked pointedly.

"Don't be silly, Rose, this is fine. I had a big sandwich for lunch while you were sleeping and I think I'm still full."

Rose smiled at Lara and said, "Cal is going into town tomorrow morning for supplies. You said this afternoon that you needed some things, Lara. Would you like to ride in with him?"

Lara froze with a forkful of fish poised in midair. She glanced at Cal, who was watching her, his face unreadable.

"I, uh, well, I don't know, I just wanted to go to the pharmacy and make a few other stops. I can drive in on my own later..."

"Don't be silly," Rose said flatly. "I'm sure Cal would welcome the company, wouldn't you, Cal?"

The hired hand, who was now as firmly on the spot as Lara had been a moment earlier, hesitated just a second before saying smoothly, "Sure, why not?"

But he didn't look at Lara as he said it.

"What time?" Lara offered resignedly, conceding defeat.

"Is nine okay?" Cal asked, finally meeting her eyes.

"Fine." Lara rose and carried her plate to the counter next to the sink. As if she had given some sort of signal, Cal did the same. When he returned to the table and picked up a platter, Rose said loudly,

"Shoo, shoo!" She flapped her hands as if scattering chickens. "Do we have to go through this every night, Cal? I'm perfectly capable of cleaning my own kitchen. Now just clear off and let me make the coffee."

Cal smiled slightly. "Thanks for dinner," he said, and headed out through the screen door. Lara watched through the window as he sat on the top step of the back porch and lit a cigarette, leaning back on his elbows and gazing up at the darkening sky.

Rose came to stand beside Lara, turning on the tap as she rinsed her plate.

"Did you have to do that?" Lara whispered to her urgently, aware of the open window over the sink.

"Do what?" Rose said mildly.

"Come on, Rose! It was obvious the man didn't want to take me with him tomorrow, and now he's being forced into it."

"I don't know what you're talking about, Lara Marie, I was just being practical and Cal has no trouble speaking up for himself. If he didn't want to take you he would have said so."

Lara couldn't tell if her grandmother's innocence was real or feigned, but at the moment it didn't matter. The trip to town was on, and she would just have to make the best of it.

Rose made coffee as Lara loaded the dishwasher. Then Rose said in a tired voice, "I'm going into the den to watch my game show, honey. Would you finish up here and bring Cal a cup of coffee when it's ready? He takes it black."

Lara shot her grandmother an exasperated glance, but Rose was already walking out of the room.

Lara sighed and flicked the switch on the dishwasher, then sat and watched the coffeemaker spew steaming, dark brown liquid into the clear glass pot as the dishwasher churned noisily. When the coffeepot was full she got a mug from the cabinet and filled it with the fragrant brew. As she pushed through the screen door Cal looked up and saw the cup in her hand.

"Thanks," he said, as she gave it to him. "None for you?"

"I'm trying to give it up. I'm down to two cups in the morning," Lara replied.

He glanced at the cigarette burning down between his fingers and said, "Java's just one of my bad habits."

Lara didn't want to pursue that line of conversation, so she said nothing.

"I'm glad you came out here to stay with your grandmother," Cal said suddenly. "I've been worried about her."

Lara looked at him.

"I know it's none of my business," he added hastily, reading her expression, "but I see her all the time and she always seems so beat..." His voice trailed off and stopped.

"I'm bringing Rose to see her doctor as soon as she'll agree to the trip," Lara said stiffly. "It may take some persuasion but I'll get her there."

"Good."

"I would have been here sooner but I had to finish

up at my job,'' Lara added, as if he deserved an explanation.

''What's your job?''

''I'm a kindergarten teacher at an elementary school outside Chicago.''

He stood, dropped the cigarette to the ground and then crushed it under his heel. ''That's nice. Kids that age are real cute.''

A cool breeze caressed them as he picked up the butt and tossed it into Rose's plastic-lined trash can. ''Your grandmother told me I could smoke but she didn't want to be stepping on any dirty butts,'' he said, and grinned.

Lara stared at him, drawn to the full smile she hadn't seen earlier. He had large, white teeth that seemed even whiter against the background of his deeply tanned face.

She looked down, breaking eye contact with him. ''Thanks for bringing my suitcases into the guest room.''

''You're welcome. I do most of the lifting that Rose can't manage.''

''I could have done it.''

''It was no problem,'' he said gently, as if wondering why she was making such a big deal out of it.

Lara began to wonder about it herself. Did it make her uncomfortable to see how invaluable he had become to her grandmother in such a short time? There was something unnerving about the whole situation. Why didn't it occur to Rose that the incomparable Cal might just be too good to be true?

Cal cleared his throat. "Well, I guess I'll be going," he said. "I'll see you here in the morning."

Lara watched him lope across the wide field that separated the main house from the stable. He had an easy, swinging stride that seemed to eat up the ground.

Lara turned and went back into the house.

That night, Cal could not sleep. Long after all the lights were off in the main house he prowled the confines of the loft, finally abandoning his tiny, hot apartment for the outdoors. He crossed dew-laden grass under a nearly full moon, heading for the pond behind the paddocks where the hands sometimes watered the horses.

The surface of the water was completely still, making it resemble a mirror. He stripped off his jeans and dove into the refreshing natural pool, swimming until he felt tired enough to relax.

He climbed onto the bank and collapsed, pushing his wet hair out of his eyes. He fumbled in the pocket of his discarded pants for a cigarette, then lay back against the verdant bank, lighting up and inhaling deeply.

He knew the reason for his restlessness: Rose's granddaughter was on his mind.

For almost two months the Daniels ranch had been the perfect place to hide out and keep a low profile, but the arrival of the tall, cool blonde from Chicago presented an unforeseen complication. He didn't know what he had been expecting, perhaps a younger, marcelled clone of her grandmother, but since he met Lara he hadn't been able to put her out of his thoughts.

Lara. She was named after the indomitable heroine of *Doctor Zhivago.* Had her mom been a Russian literature buff? Or just a fan of weepy movies? He smiled to himself, but then sobered quickly, studying his cigarette by moonlight as a thin wisp of smoke trailed lazily from its glowing end.

The knowledge that Lara would be around for the rest of the summer disturbed him. He was much too attracted to her; he had felt the connection the moment he saw her. She was very pretty, but it was more than just her looks. There was a sweetness about her, a candid quality that contrasted sharply with his recent life and reminded him of previous happiness, once enjoyed and now lost. He found her air of forthright innocence as alluring as the scent of a seductive perfume.

Would he be able to see this girl every day and stay away from her?

He sat up, watching a transparent cloud drift past the moon. Maybe he should just pick up and go, give Rose some excuse and hit the road. It would be safer than staying, but he had to admit to himself that he was reluctant to leave. It wasn't just that he was fond of the old lady, who had been good to him. He was also tired of running, tired of the featureless faces of strangers, tired of interchangeable rooms in cheap motels and having no place to call his own. He had found a haven in Rose's kindness and a steady job. He was reluctant to lose either one.

But the problem of the girl remained.

He would have to avoid her, but he could see already that Rose was going to be a problem. She clearly thought of both younger people as her adjuncts and saw nothing wrong with sending them off on joint errands, like the trip into town. He would be forced to walk a fine line, going along with Rose's plans but at the same limiting his contact with Lara.

He exhaled a plume of grayish smoke. He could do it, he thought. He had learned to police himself through grim experience. He would keep Lara at a polite distance and stay a while longer, save some money to see him through the lean times sure to come.

He stood and looked around at this place he was not ready to forsake for the open road, at the refuge that had sheltered him after so much running.

He slipped into his jeans and walked back to the loft.

Two

In the morning Lara ate breakfast with Rose and then finished her unpacking while waiting for Cal to arrive. She heard him come into the house as she slipped a stack of underwear into a drawer.

Lara glanced into the mirror above the dresser. She had washed her hair that morning and now it fell loosely around her shoulders, contrasting with the sapphire blue blouse which emphasized her eyes. Just a trace of powder dusted her cheeks and she excused the lipstick on her mouth as a concession to her grandmother, who thought women weren't dressed without it.

Lara couldn't admit to herself that she wanted to look attractive for Rose's hired hand.

Cal was waiting in the kitchen, dressed in tan chino pants and a plaid cotton shirt with the sleeves rolled up to his elbows. His glance swept over Lara's short denim skirt and slim bare legs, then rested on her face.

"Ready to go?" he said shortly.

Lara nodded.

"Do you have the list I gave you?" Rose asked him. She was standing at the counter, folding eggs into a bowl of cake batter.

"Yes, ma'am," Cal replied. "We'll be back in a couple of hours."

Rose nodded, absorbed in her recipe.

Cal held the screen door for Lara, and as she stepped past him she caught a whiff of soap and lime shaving cream.

Ron's old pickup stood in front of the house, its dented fenders and rusted chrome reflecting long years of service.

"Is that thing mobile?" Lara said doubtfully.

"It runs. I've been working on it. I replaced the shock absorbers, the alternator belt and the distributor last week."

Of course, Lara thought dryly. Was there anything this man couldn't do?

Cal gave her his hand to help her up into the cab, and she fairly flew into the seat. He was very strong and she found that alluring. She bit her lip and stared straight ahead, annoyed with herself. She couldn't seem to stop her thoughts from taking a personal turn regarding him, and each lapse made her more determined to exercise self-discipline.

Cal slid onto the seat next to her and started the truck. It lurched forward and he said, "Sorry. I'm still working on the engine timing, I don't think all the pistons are firing right.''

Lara hadn't the faintest idea what he was talking about, but she nodded sagely.

''I guess you haven't seen the town in a while,'' he observed, turning out of the driveway and onto the access road.

''Not since my last visit when I was a teenager.''

''Well, a new bar opened last month, that was big news,'' he said, shooting her a sidelong glance.

Lara couldn't help smiling in response.

''It's called the Big Sky Rest, but I haven't seen anybody resting in there,'' he said dryly.

Lara grinned. ''I always found the local names confusing. Why is the town named Red Springs? There are no red springs, in fact there aren't any springs of any color.''

''There used to be. Back in Indian times there were hot springs out near the reservation, but they dried up when the water table fell in the late eighteen hundreds. The Blackfeet called the springs red because they used to geyser around sunset and the water seemed to take on the color of the sky.''

Lara stared at him. ''How do you know that?''

He shrugged. ''I asked.''

Feeling slightly silly, Lara said, ''I never did. The last time I was here my only concern was whether my high school boyfriend back home in Illinois was going to wait for me over the summer.''

''And did he?''

''No,'' Lara replied, laughing.

''That's hard to believe.''

"Believe it. He spent ten weeks with another lifeguard at the pool where he worked and then expected to resume with me when she went back to college in the fall."

"What did you do?"

"I threw his high school ring into the Mississippi River."

He grinned. "Good!"

"Yeah, I really enjoyed that. That is, until his mother called mine and demanded the sixty bucks she had paid for it."

Cal chuckled. "What did your mother say?"

"She said she'd tally up the cost of all the meals Tim had eaten at my house, deduct sixty dollars from it, and then send Tim's father the bill."

"I guess that was the end of the discussion."

"It was, but I was still angry with my parents. They forced me to come out here for the summer and I knew what Tim was like—he wasn't going to spend that time working on his tan. The way I saw it, the whole thing was their fault, not Tim's."

"If he couldn't wait for you he didn't deserve you," Cal said quietly.

Lara glanced over at him, but said nothing.

"What's Tim doing today?" Cal asked.

"He's in divinity school," Lara said, deadpan.

Cal looked at her in amazement.

"It's true. He had a conversion or something."

"Well, at least you know he'll understand the sinners who come to him asking for forgiveness," Cal said, and Lara laughed.

The hot, bumpy trip to town somehow seemed

very short and pleasant. Lara found Cal easy to talk to, even though he didn't say much; he was that rarity of rarities—a good listener. She found herself chattering on while he did little more than comment on what she said, but by the time they reached the dusty square in the center of town she had lost the reserve she had promised herself to maintain.

Cal pulled up in front of the feed store and said, "I have to go in here for some supplies. Will you be okay?"

Lara nodded. "I want to stop at the pharmacy and then at the package store for Rose's beer."

"Does her doctor say she can drink that?"

Lara sighed. "Yes. Believe me, I've asked him. He says it won't hurt her and it relaxes her or something," she replied irritably.

"I gather you disagree."

"Does it seem like a good idea to let a seventy-eight-year-old stroke victim guzzle beer?" Lara demanded.

"She doesn't guzzle it—she has a can or two with dinner," Cal replied. "I've never seen her drunk."

"Now you sound like Dr. Ponter."

"Do you want me to get the brew? Some of the characters who hang out at the package store aren't the best."

"Don't be ridiculous, I'll be fine," Lara said briskly, turning to yank the door handle at her side. Nothing happened.

"That sticks, let me get it for you," Cal said, exiting the cab from his side and jumping lightly to the ground. He came around and opened Lara's door from the outside.

"Sorry, this is one more thing I have to fix," Cal said, as he gave Lara his hand and helped her down to the street. "I haven't had many passengers so I've let it go."

They stood facing each other on the bright sidewalk, Cal squinting into the sun.

"Half an hour?" he said, and she nodded.

Lara crossed the street to the pharmacy as he went into the feed store behind them.

The drugstore had been redone since Lara's last visit. The old-fashioned soda fountain was gone, replaced by a modern counter and leatherette booths, and the wooden shelves had given way to glass-enclosed displays. Lara filled a prescription for her grandmother and then bought some toiletries for herself, adding a new lipstick and a tube of mascara as an afterthought. She stopped off next door for some groceries and then stowed her purchases in the back of the waiting truck. With about ten minutes remaining before she had to meet Cal she set off down the street, nodding at the few people who were on the main thoroughfare at midmorning.

The package store was cool, and empty except for the clerk. Lara bought two six-packs and then left with them under her arm, stopping short as a long shadow crossed her path in the doorway.

"Well hello, little lady," a masculine voice said. "What you got there?"

Lara looked up into the friendly, if too close, face of a young man about her age who was blocking her path. He was dressed in jeans and a Western-cut shirt with a ten-gallon hat set back on his head.

"Excuse me," Lara said, and tried to brush past him.

He put a hand on her shoulder to detain her. "What you doing buying that stuff at this hour of the morning?" he asked pleasantly. Too pleasantly. He did not appear to be drunk, but on the other hand, he wasn't moving out of her way.

"I'm very busy," Lara said, looking desperately up the street, which had suddenly become as deserted as a mall lot at midnight. Cal was nowhere in sight.

"Too busy for a friendly chat with ole Jerry?"

"Yes."

"That's not a very neighborly attitude," he replied. "You must be new around here—I'd have remembered seeing you."

"I'm visiting," Lara said shortly, taking a step to the side. He stepped with her.

"Visiting who?"

"None of your business," Lara snapped, tiring of the game. She looked back into the store; the clerk had vanished also.

"I know just about everybody around here," the man said. "I bet we have a few acquaintances in common."

"I doubt it." Lara's heart leapt suddenly when she saw Cal emerge from the feed store with a large bag slung over his shoulder. He didn't notice her until he had dropped it onto the flatbed, but then she saw him look up the street and spot her as he straightened. He started walking toward her immediately.

The surge of relief Lara felt was all out of proportion to the circumstances. Her companion had done little more than talk, after all, and she hardly knew Cal much better than the man who was blocking her path. Yet she couldn't help fastening her gaze on Cal's beseechingly as he appeared behind her assailant's shoulder.

"You okay, Lara?" Cal asked.

The other man whirled to face Cal. "Who the hell are you?" he demanded, his tone a lot less friendly now.

"What's it matter?" Cal replied evenly. "I'm a lot bigger than you are."

"Get lost, buddy. Me and the young lady here were having a little chat."

"She doesn't look like she's enjoying the conversation." Cal motioned to Lara and said, "Lara, come over here."

Lara scuttled behind him as the two men squared off, facing each other. Cal swept her back with one long arm as she started forward again anxiously.

"Let's go, Cal," Lara said, tugging on his wrist. "It's stupid to have a confrontation over this. Nothing happened."

He looked down at her consideringly, nodded, then turned to go, taking her burden from her. Just as he glanced away the other man swung hard at him with a wild roundhouse, but missed.

Cal dropped his package and whirled, decking Jerry with one punch, and the man crumpled bonelessly to the sidewalk. The package store clerk showed up at the door, glanced through it at the prone and senseless body and rushed back inside.

Lara stood with both hands clamped over her mouth, her eyes wide with alarm, as Cal knelt next to Jerry and felt his pulse.

"Is he all right?" she whispered.

"Yeah, he's just out," Cal replied quietly.

"What are we going to do?" she said. "We can't just leave him here."

"I'll try to bring him around," Cal said. "Go and get some ice inside."

A small crowd was gathering, drawn by the sight of a grown man sprawled full-length in the street, with, amazingly, his hat still on his head. Lara took it off and set it next to him before going back into the store.

"Can you let me have some ice?" she said to the clerk.

He put some into a plastic bag and handed it to her.

"May I use your phone?"

"Sure, but I already called the sheriff," he said.

Lara stared at him, dismayed.

"Why did you do that?" she demanded.

"Lady, I can't have no brawls at my place of business," he said.

"This wasn't a brawl, this was one punch! There's no reason to make a federal case out of it."

He shrugged. "Whatever. Sheriff's on his way."

Lara ran outside just as the county car, its blue light pulsing, glided silently to the curb.

Cal was frozen in place, staring at it. He didn't even look at Lara as she came to his side.

The door with the large blue star on it opened slowly, and a figure clad entirely in khaki emerged, surveying the scene. Lara thought the slight, sandy haired man looked vaguely familiar as he walked over to the prone figure and nodded wearily.

"Jerry Perkins," he said. "What a surprise. What did he do this time?"

Cal was silent, so Lara said hastily, "It was really nothing, Sheriff—"

"Then how come Jerry here is out cold?" the sheriff asked, interrupting her.

"He stopped me in the street and wouldn't let me pass. Mr. Winston here came to help me and...Jerry took a swing at him."

"And?"

"He missed and, Cal, Mr. Winston, hit him."

The sheriff looked at Cal. "You the guy working out at the Daniels place?" he asked.

Cal nodded.

"I recognized the truck," the sheriff said.

"It happened just as this young lady says, Bob," the clerk announced from his doorway. "I came out from the storeroom right when this second fella arrived. It sure looked to me like Jerry threw the first punch, and it would be like him to pester this girl."

"I'm Lara Daniels, Rose's granddaughter," Lara chimed in helpfully.

"I thought you were," the sheriff said. "You don't remember me, do you? Bob Trask...I used to work summers for your uncle Ron. We met that year you came out here with your parents when you were in high school."

Lara smiled broadly, grasping Trask's extended hand. "Of course I remember you. I'm sorry we have to meet again under such awkward circumstances."

Jerry moaned and turned his head.

"Oh, that's just old Jerry," Trask said, releasing Lara's hand and bending over the prostrate man. "He's always annoying somebody."

"I have some ice here," Lara said, proferring the bag.

"Good idea. I have to wake him up. I got a kit in the car." Bob went to the sedan and returned with a medic box in his hand, while Cal watched him tensely.

Since the sheriff arrived he hadn't said a word.

Bob uncapped a bottle of smelling salts and held the vial under Jerry's nose. Jerry stirred and coughed, then his eyes opened.

"He'll be okay," Bob assured them. "I'll take him over to the jail and let him cool off until he's ready to go home. Won't be the first time he's spent some time with us."

"Then there won't be any charges filed?" Lara asked, aware of Cal's stone face and wary demeanor.

Bob shook his head. "If I filed formal assault charges every time Jerry got into a fight the paperwork would keep me from doing anything else."

Lara saw Cal relax visibly; he seemed to exhale silently, and his clenched fists opened.

"You will have to fill out an incident report, though." He looked over at the package store clerk, who was hovering in the background. "I'll get your version later, Larry, okay?"

Larry nodded and went back inside.

"You people go on about your business," Bob said, making dispersing gestures to the eight or ten onlookers who were hanging around the sidewalk. "There's nothing to see here."

Bob crouched next to Jerry as the townspeople drifted away. There was a purpling bruise growing on the side of Jerry's face. Bob touched it and Jerry yelped.

"He's coming around," Bob announced. "Winston, can you give me a hand here? I want to load him into the car."

The two men carried the mumbling Jerry to the back seat of the sedan. Bob put the ice in a towel and propped it under Jerry's swelling jaw.

"Couple cups of coffee and he'll be okay," Bob said. "You two want to follow me over to the jail? The form is short, it should only take a few minutes. Unless you want to consider filing a civil assault suit against Jerry, Mr. Winston. You've got two witnesses who say he started it, but he might try to countersue, since he was the one on the ground."

Cal shook his head.

"Okay," Bob said, bringing his hands together smartly. "I'll see the both of you in a few minutes."

He climbed into the car and drove off, with Jerry slumped in the back seat.

Lara looked at Cal, who was following the departing police car with his eyes. "Cat got your tongue?" she asked.

He glanced at her inquiringly.

"You haven't said a word since Bob Trask arrived."

"I don't like cops," he said shortly.

"I guess not. But it should be apparent, even to you, that this one is giving you a break. You did hit that man and knock him out. Bob could make trouble for you if he wanted to pursue it."

Cal grunted.

"Should we go over to the jail now and make the report?" Lara asked.

He didn't answer, merely walked with her to the pickup and drove the several blocks to the Linton County Sheriff's local station. Inside, Bob Trask was waiting for them, and they spent fifteen minutes answering questions so that Trask could file his report.

Lara was struck by Cal's changed attitude; the relaxed, bantering person who had driven her into Red Springs had been replaced by a cautious, almost unresponsive stranger. He replied in monosyllables to Trask's questions and never offered more information than was requested. When Trask finished and walked them to the door, Cal went ahead and waited in the hall as Lara turned to say goodbye.

"How long are you staying with your grandmother?" Trask asked Lara.

"Until September."

"Do you mind if I give you a call there at the ranch? Maybe we could get together."

Lara looked at the back of Cal's head. He appeared to be reading a bulletin board and ignoring them.

"Sure," Lara said. "The number's in the book."

Trask beamed. "You'll hear from me soon," he said, as Lara walked out into corridor.

When Cal turned and saw her he went ahead without a word. As they were stepping into the street he said, "You dated that cop when you were a kid?"

"Not really. We had a few Cokes, I think we went to a summer league ball game. I was being faithful to Tim, remember?"

"So are you going to be dating Trask now?"

Lara stared at him, but he didn't look away. "I have no idea," she finally said frostily. "Maybe."

He helped her into the truck and then jumped into the cab himself, turning the key in the ignition without looking at her again.

The trip back to the ranch was very different from the trip to town. Lara's encounter with Jerry Perkins had cast a pall on the morning; Cal spoke only when spoken to on the drive home until she finally gave up and stopped talking to him. Even more disturbing, she had the helpless feeling that her encounter with Jerry Perkins had little to do with Cal's reaction. He had seemed fine and in control, if annoyed by Perkins's behavior, until Bob Trask arrived. Then Cal had turned into a statue.

"What have you got against the police?" Lara asked suddenly, as he stopped the truck in front of her grandmother's house.

Cal stared straight ahead, then turned to look at her. "My foster father was killed by police about twenty years ago."

Lara didn't respond, startled into silence.

"His union went on strike," Cal continued. "He

was out on the picket line with his buddies, and the company brought some scabs through to take their jobs. A fight broke out and the cops were called. When my father resisted arrest, he caught a billy club to the side of his head. He died in the emergency room an hour later."

"How awful," Lara murmured.

"The cop, by the way, was charged with nothing. Cleared by the review board. Internal Affairs ruled it an accidental death in the line of duty."

"Where was this?"

"Does it matter?" Cal countered, yanking the keys from the ignition. "You asked me a question and I answered it."

"But surely you see that Bob Trask isn't responsible—" Lara began, but he held up his hand.

"The uniform makes me jumpy, okay? And if you had my experiences you would feel the same."

"What experiences? What else happened to you? You mentioned a foster father, were you an orphan?"

"I was abandoned at a convent when I was an infant," Cal said shortly. "I never knew my biological parents, the foster parents who took me in when I was ten are both dead now. The man who was killed was the only father I ever knew."

"I'm sorry. You must have had a difficult childhood."

"Talking about it won't change anything," he said, and jumped down from the truck. When he came around to help her out the door his fixed expression indicated that the discussion was over.

Her mind teeming with questions, Lara followed Cal as he went back into the house carrying Rose's beer.

Rose was waiting for them in the front hall. "Phone call for you," she said to Lara. "I heard the truck pull up and told him to hang on. It's Bob Trask."

"Not wasting any time, is he?" Cal said quietly in a sarcastic tone. He went ahead of her to put the beer in the kitchen as Lara took the phone.

"Bob?" she said.

"Hi, Lara. I hope I'm not rushing things, but I just had a change of plans and I have the weekend off. I wondered if you would like to join me for dinner on Friday night?"

Lara heard the kitchen door slam as Cal exited through the back of the house. Something about that forceful, ringing bang made the decision for her.

"Sure," she said. "What time?"

"I'll pick you up at six. Does Thomasina's here in town sound okay?"

"That sounds fine, but I should tell you that I can't stay out too late. I'd like to be back before ten to keep an eye on Rose."

"That's fine."

"Okay. I'll see you then."

Lara hung up the phone to find her grandmother standing right behind her.

"Have you got a date?" Rose asked.

"I'm having dinner with Bob at Thomasina's on Friday. I wouldn't call it a date."

"What would you call it?" Rose said, grinning.

"A reunion of two old friends."

Rose chuckled.

"What's so funny, Rose? I ran into him in town and he recognized me. If you would rather I stayed here with you, just say so."

"I wouldn't dream of interfering with your social life," Rose said airily. "Cal and I will just have to muddle through dinner on our own. Did you get what you wanted in town?"

"Yes, thanks. I have your prescription—Dr. Ponter said you should start on it right away." Lara fished in her purse and handed Rose the bottle.

Rose examined it with distaste. "I'm taking so many pills I should rattle when I walk." She went over to the sink to run water into a glass.

"You have to visit him soon, Rose," Lara said firmly.

"Who?" Rose asked innocently, uncapping the bottle.

"Dr. Ponter," Lara replied. "I'm going to see if he can fit you in Monday."

"Oh, all right," Rose said irritably, swallowing a tricolored capsule. "You're a worse bully than your uncle Ron, and he could have given lessons in the fine art of pushing people around."

"Why don't you sit down and I'll make lunch," Lara suggested, eager to change the subject now that Rose had agreed to see the doctor. "Then you can take your nap."

Rose sat obediently, and Lara began to set the table.

* * *

The next several days passed uneventfully, with Lara absorbed in her accounting and Rose busy with the household routine. Lara noticed that her grandmother had become forgetful, leaving chores half finished and neglecting to perform standard tasks like defrosting food and putting perishables back into the refrigerator. Lara followed after Rose, silently rectifying situations, but her concern grew as she saw that her grandmother was not as independent as she pretended to be.

Cal was a solid presence as he came and went, going about his work, showing up for dinner every night freshly washed and combed. Lara found herself looking for him, listening for his step, watching through the window as he walked across a field, long legs pumping, shouldering whatever burden he was carrying easily. She always stopped when she realized she was staring, but that didn't prevent her from being drawn in again the next time he ambled into view.

At five-thirty on Friday Lara took a shower and changed into a shirtwaist dress, brushing her damp hair and donning earrings and a gold necklace. Rose was puttering around in the kitchen, making dinner, as Bob Trask pulled up in front of the house in a late-model sports car.

Lara went to the door and let him in, accepting the bunch of flowers he offered somewhat uneasily. It was clear that even if she wanted to view this as a friendly dinner, Bob had a more romantic agenda on his mind.

"Where's your grandmother?" Bob asked. "I haven't seen her in a while and I'd like to say hello."

Lara led him inside and put the flowers in a vase while Bob chatted with Rose. Lara was just turning to go when Cal trotted up the steps and tapped on the back door.

"Come on in, Cal," Rose trilled.

Cal entered the kitchen and took in Lara's dress, her visitor and the vase full of flowers in one glance.

"Cal, you know Bob Trask," Lara said smoothly, praying that neither man would mention the encounter with Jerry Perkins in front of her grandmother.

Cal nodded at Bob and then sat at the table. Rose put a glass of iced tea in front of him and Cal seized it gratefully, as if glad of something to do.

"Well, I guess we'd better get going, the reservation is for six-thirty," Bob said.

"You two kids have a good time," Rose chirped, and Lara shot her a dark glance. Was it Lara's imagination or was Rose enjoying the slightly uncomfortable situation of one young man watching her granddaughter go off on a date with another?

"Take your second pill before you eat, Rose," Lara called over her shoulder.

"Nag, nag, nag," Rose replied, but Lara saw her reach for the bottle as she left.

The drive to Red Springs seemed to take much longer than it had with Cal, even though Lara's transportation this time was much more comfortable than Ron's dilapidated pickup. She made small talk with Bob, catching up on what he had been doing for the last decade: graduating from high school, attending the police academy, starting out on the local force before moving up to the county sheriff's department. By the time they reached Thomasina's Lara remembered why she had liked him as a teenager: he had retained the same sunny, engaging manner she recalled from their earlier acquaintance.

Thomasina's had changed as little as had Bob. The checkered tablecloths, wine bottles in wicker baskets and hanging plants were all the same. They were seated and ordered, and as they ate their salad Bob brought up the subject of Lara's companion that afternoon for the first time.

"That guy Cal been working for your grandmother long?" Bob asked, forking romaine lettuce into his mouth.

"A couple of months, I think. Why?"

"I just wondered. I've seen him coming into town for supplies. Never has much to say for himself."

"Rose tells me he's hardworking and reliable."

"He sure as hell wasn't happy about giving that statement the other day."

"I think he just wanted to forget the whole thing. It didn't seem worth an incident report."

Bob nodded. "Where's he from, do you know?"

"I have no idea. I just got here myself and I really haven't asked him many questions."

"Well, I guess there's no reason to interrogate him, since he hasn't been causing any trouble." Bob smiled suddenly. "Jerry went home about three hours after I took him to the jail. He's going to need some dental work—I think your friend chipped his tooth with that punch."

"I wish the whole thing had never happened."

Bob shrugged. "Jerry just asks for trouble. He can't take no for an answer."

The waiter came and cleared the table, then brought the main course. Bob launched into a description of a recent case he had handled, which carried them through to dessert. He then suggested going on to a nightspot in Sadler, a bigger town about fifteen minutes farther north, but Lara reminded him that she wanted to get back home to check on Rose. Bob was obviously disappointed, but settled for a commitment to a date for the following weekend. He drove Lara back by a route that took a little longer, regaling her with police anecdotes the whole time, but she was still home by a little after nine-thirty.

She went directly to Rose's room, and her heart leapt into her throat when she saw that the door was ajar and Rose's bed was empty. Lara ran into the kitchen, where she found a note propped against the sugar bowl.

> "Took Rose to County General—she passed out after dinner. Call me there."

It was signed simply, "Cal." The large block letters swam before Lara's eyes as she grabbed for the phone and got the number from information. She was transferred several times once she reached the hospital, her pulse racing, until she finally talked to the cardiac unit floor nurse. The woman told her that Rose had been brought into the emergency room and then admitted to the cardiac unit. Dr. Ponter had been in to see her and she was "resting comfortably," whatever that meant. Ponter was now visiting some other patients, but would be available to talk to Lara if she came in during the next hour.

"The man who brought my grandmother in to the emergency room, is he still there?" Lara asked anxiously.

"Tall, dark and handsome?" the nurse asked wisely.

"Yes."

"He's waiting in the lounge across the hall."

"May I speak to him?"

"Hang on." There was a pause of dead air on the line, and then Lara's eyes closed gratefully as she heard Cal's deep voice say her name inquiringly.

"Oh, Cal, is she okay?" Lara whispered.

"Yes, yes, she's fine. I'm sorry I had to leave you that short note, but at the time I didn't know what was going on and I just wanted to get her to the hospital. She had a reaction to the new medicine, it lowered her blood pressure too much and she passed out, but she was already awake by the time she arrived here. Her doctor wanted to keep her overnight for observation in view of her age and her history, but he told me he didn't think she was in any immediate danger."

"I feel so guilty," Lara said, her eyes filling. "I should have been there. I knew she had been on that new protocol just a few days, I shouldn't have gone out and left her alone."

"She wasn't alone," Cal said quietly.

"But what if it had happened after you left for the

evening? She would have fainted on the floor in an empty house—'' Lara stopped, too upset to continue.

''That didn't happen so it's pointless to torture yourself about it,'' Cal said evenly. ''And don't speed on your way here and have an accident, Rose is fine. She's just sleeping. They gave her intravenous fluids to raise her blood pressure and she responded right away. Her pressure is normal now.''

Lara sighed with relief. ''I'll make the trip in half an hour,'' she said.

''Forty minutes,'' he said, correcting her.

''All right. Will you wait?''

''Of course,'' he said quietly, and the steady reassurance in his voice made her glad he would be there when she arrived.

Lara's drive to the hospital passed in a blur. She had only the vaguest recollection of Sadler, but found the hospital after just one wrong turn; the way was clearly marked by road signs. The cardiac unit was on the third floor, and Cal was standing in the hall as the elevator doors opened.

Lara had to restrain herself from running to him. One part of her knew it was ridiculous to feel so confident in someone she had just met, but another part, the atavistic core of her being where the most basic feelings dominated, sensed that she could trust Cal Winston.

He took both of her hands and said, ''She's okay, really. Your timing is perfect, the doctor just went into her room.'' He pointed to the door.

Lara released him and fled down the corridor,

waiting patiently until the doctor emerged from the darkened cubicle.

"Dr. Ponter, I'm Lara Daniels," she said, extending her hand. "We've talked on the phone."

"Oh, yes, how are you?" the doctor said, shaking her hand. He was middle-aged and direct, with a pair of glasses shoved up into his graying hair. "Your grandmother is doing much better, but we plan to run some tests in the morning to determine why she had such an adverse reaction to the medication."

"Do you know exactly what happened?"

"Apparently she suffered an episode of hypotension, which caused an insufficient supply of blood to the brain and she passed out. I can only tell you that the new medicine I gave her is no stronger than the last one, and she had been doing fine on it for four days. This could have happened if she got mixed up and took too much of it at once, or took the doses too close together." He hesitated, and Lara sensed that he wanted to say something more.

"Or?" she prompted.

"Or her heart could just be weakening, its pumping action decreased," the doctor said gently. "But I wouldn't jump to that conclusion. It was probably the medicine. We'll know more tomorrow."

Lara thought about it. Could Rose have forgotten taking the pill as Lara left with Bob and taken another later? It was possible, even probable, given her distracted nature since the onset of her medical problems.

She would have to be watched even more closely.

"I'd like to stay over in town so you can call me if anything happens tonight," Lara said.

"That's really not necessary. She's completely stabilized now and she's on a monitor that will alert us immediately if her blood pressure or heart pattern changes. She'll just sleep until morning. You should go home and do the same. You can call me first thing for the report."

Lara looked at him doubtfully.

"If it were my grandmother I'd go home to bed," the doctor said. "Hanging around here will accomplish nothing."

Lara sighed and nodded.

"We'll talk in the morning," the doctor said, and strode off down the hall.

Lara went into the room and saw Rose sleeping in the bed, looking very tiny, as if she were a prematurely aged doll. The older woman was swallowed up in the white bed, the monitor at her side flashing numbers. Lara stood there for as long as she could take it, then walked away.

Cal was standing just where she had left him. She started to walk toward him, then stopped, reaction to the sudden episode setting in all at once. She shivered and wrapped her arms around her torso, leaning against the wall.

Cal was at her side immediately; his arm slipped around her waist protectively.

"You okay?" he said, bending to put his lips next to her ear.

Lara nodded mutely, too overcome with emotion

to speak. She turned slightly and in the next instant she was in his arms.

Cal held her tightly, cradling her head against his shoulder, his silent support more comforting than the most eloquent words could have been. She was aware of the slim muscularity of his body, his height and the masculine scent she had noticed before, then stepped back as someone tapped her.

"I'm sorry to interrupt," the floor nurse said, "but Dr. Ponter wanted to make sure you had the number of his pager." She handed Lara a slip of paper.

"Thanks," Lara said, and then looked back at Cal, who was watching her closely.

"It's just that I'm all she has," she whispered, wiping her eyes with the back of her hand.

He nodded.

"I didn't realize that she was this sick, or I would have been here earlier. I could have taken a leave of absence. The specialist said a lot of things I didn't understand, you know that double-talk doctors use. Or maybe I didn't want to believe she was so ill. Her letters and phone calls were always so...cheerful." She bit her lip.

Cal put his hand on her shoulder. "None of that matters now. You just have to do what you can for her from this moment on, right?"

"Right," Lara echoed hoarsely.

"We both will." His fingers squeezed her gently, then he looked around him. "Let's get out of here. You'll feel better once you're away from this antiseptic atmosphere."

They rode down in the elevator with a man who

was reading a pamphlet on the postnatal care of infants. They crossed the tiled lobby and went through the double glass doors to the parking lot. Lara took a deep breath of the balmy night air.

"Better?" Cal said.

Lara nodded shakily.

"Still feeling a little rocky?"

"Just a little."

"I think I should drive you home."

"In the truck?" Lara asked.

"No, I'll leave the pickup here and come back for it with one of the hands tomorrow. Let's take your car, it should find a few less ruts in the roads."

"I wouldn't count on that," Lara replied dryly, as they walked toward it.

"You've got the keys?" Cal asked.

Lara handed them to him, only too happy to have him take over so she could collapse in the passenger seat. She closed her eyes as the car glided onto the street. She just listened to the hum of the engine as they rode until Cal's voice asked softly, "Are you asleep?"

Lara turned her head to look at him. "No."

"It's okay if you want to sack out. There won't be any questions about the route. I'm not giving a test at the end."

Lara smiled for the first time that night since she saw Rose's empty bed and knew that something was wrong. "How do you like driving my limousine?" she asked.

"It beats the pickup, but that's not saying much."

Lara chuckled. "You didn't have a car when you came here?"

"Nope. I sold it on the road when I ran out of money."

"The road from where?"

"Anywhere and everywhere," he said evasively.

"Do you like living like that?"

He looked over at her, his expression sober. "It reduces complications," he replied.

"Like becoming too fond of a sickly old lady?" Lara suggested pointedly.

"Becoming too fond of anybody is always risky," he said simply, and Lara felt a chill at the finality of his tone.

He drove the rest of the way back in silence, and when they reached the house he walked up to the door with Lara, who turned to him on the porch.

"I can't thank you enough..." she began, then stopped as he put his finger to her lips.

"You don't have to say anything, Lara," he murmured. "I understand."

Lara stood on tiptoe impulsively to kiss his cheek, and as she drew back he put his hands on her shoulders. Lara looked up at him, yearning toward him as the current between them sparked and grew, blanking out the night sounds and leaving them alone with the rush of their own breathing.

He stepped away suddenly, and it was over.

"Good night," he said, and turned instantly, running quickly down the steps.

Lara watched him go, swallowing her wrenching disappointment as her respiration returned to normal.

Why had he left? Was he concerned that he was responding so strongly to a virtual stranger?

The passage of time didn't really matter. Sometimes it took only a moment to know.

But Cal was still gone.

Lara went slowly into the empty house, feeling the silence surround her. It didn't seem right that Rose was spending the night elsewhere; Lara associated her so closely with this home that she was unable to think of her grandmother existing in a different place. She walked past Rose's room quickly and went to her own, undressing in the dark and falling across the bed.

Too much had happened in one evening. She was exhausted, but the memory of Cal's rough cheek under her mouth kept her on the edge of slumber.

She felt again his hands on her shoulders, his lips against her ear. As she drifted she imagined him going further, then pushed the idea away; it was too disturbing.

She sighed deeply, and finally slept.

Cal sat bolt upright on his bed, streaming sweat, his hair plastered to his head and his muscles in knots. He looked down at his wrists as if expecting to see the handcuffs there; the nightmare had been that vivid. He swung his legs over the edge of the bed and sat with his head down and his arms across his knees, waiting for the heavy feeling of dread to pass.

When it finally did he went into the bathroom and

doused his upper body with cold water, toweling off and looking at himself in the mirror.

You have to get out of this town, he thought as he gazed at his weary, hollow-eyed image. He could feel himself being drawn toward Lara Daniels as if being sucked into a vacuum, and it would cost him his freedom if he stayed.

He went back into the other room and dropped back onto the bed, staring up at the bare beams of the loft above his head, then around at the sparsely furnished chamber. The battered chest of drawers contained his few clothes. The repainted bookshelf was piled with newspapers and magazines. The mini refrigerator and hot plate served the scant needs of a man who always ate his meals elsewhere. There were no photos or mementos. It was the home of a transient with no past and a highly questionable future.

Cal closed his eyes, calculating how much more money he would need to get to California. If he just stayed put for a few more weeks he would have enough for a bus trip there. He could lose himself in a big city, or in the rural north. Red Springs, although isolated, was just too small a town.

And it contained Lara Daniels.

He had almost kissed her; only a tremendous effort of will had pulled him away from her at the last second. He had known her just a few days and already he'd come close to breaking his cardinal rule: Don't get involved with the locals. The pattern he'd followed had kept him safe for over a year. Stop, make some money, move on, form no personal attachments. It was a safe plan but a lonely one. And somehow, once he met Lara, the loneliness that he had almost ceased to notice, like a dull headache that subsided but never went away, had suddenly become unbearable.

He was already lying to her, and if he stayed it would only get worse. When she had noticed his uneasiness around Bob Trask, he had explained it with that story about his foster father. While that was true, it was only a fraction of the history that made him unsuitable for Lara, or indeed anyone else.

If she were a different type of woman, the choice would not be difficult. He could just take his pleasure and go. But if she were a different type of woman he knew he would not be lying awake at night longing for her. She was exactly the sort of sweet, straightforward girl he had thought was lost to him forever, a woman who would run from him if she knew the secret he was harboring. The trip into Red Springs with her had made him temporarily forget the reality of his situation, but the arrival of the law in the person of Bob Trask had brought it all home to him again.

He had not expected to feel instant infatuation for anyone; he did not think of himself as that type of person. But it had happened, and he was stuck with it.

Cal rolled over on the sheet and willed himself back to sleep. He had a lot of work to do the next day. The least he could do to repay Rose's goodwill was to leave the ranch with the repairs completed.

He would have to move fast.

He didn't have much time.

Three

For the next few weeks Lara took every opportunity to see Cal, but he avoided her. If she spoke to him while he was working, he replied briefly and then moved away. At the dinners they shared he talked mostly to Rose and replied in monosyllables to Lara's questions. She began to wonder if she had done anything wrong, leaned on him too heavily at the hospital or acted too forward and scared him away. He was certainly putting a chill in the air, a neat trick since if anything it was now hotter in Red Springs than when she had arrived. And if he was around when Lara left on her dates with Bob Trask, his air of indifference was almost palpable.

Rose never did remember whether she had taken an extra pill or mislaid one the night she collapsed, but Dr. Ponter changed the medication anyhow to something administered once a day, and Lara took charge of its dispensation. The results of Rose's tests showed a deterioration of the heart muscle, and she remained weak. She spent each afternoon working on a needlepoint pillow in the den while she watched her soap operas, turning over her routine of chores to Lara, who realized she had arrived just in time to take over at home as well as with the business.

Lara ran the house and conferred with the accountant who came out from Sadler several times to help her with the ranch's books. He convinced Lara that Rose had to cut back on expenses as well as sell off some of her horses. The foreman, Jim Stampley, picked out three that were ready to go and increased the schedule of riding lessons, for which the ranch could charge twenty dollars an hour. He also cut back on his staff, releasing two part-time workers. Lara waited for him to suggest firing Cal, but apparently Cal cost little and worked a lot, so he was deemed worth saving.

July Fourth came and went. Lara attended the fireworks display in Sadler with Bob, managing to prevent him from escalating the relationship beyond a weekly date with the excuse that Rose needed constant attention. In Lara's free time she rediscovered her love of riding, exercising a mare named Goldenrod in the early morning when it was still cool. After a few days with a sore back and a sore butt, Lara got back into the rhythm of the exercise and felt as comfortable in the saddle as she had when she was seventeen.

Late one afternoon when Rose was deep in the

throes of a soap opera, Lara heard knocking on the kitchen door. She rose from the table where she had been recording a series of bank deposits and found Jim standing on the back porch.

"Hi, Jim. What's up?"

"Hi, Lara. Do you have any betadine in the house? I thought I had some in the tack room but it looks like I'm out of it. Cal was helping me with some baling wire and cut his hand on it."

"Is it bad? Does it need stitches?"

"I don't think so. It's not too deep, but he won't be able to use it for the rest of the day. I sent him back to the loft."

"Do you have any gauze and tape?" Lara asked, sensing an opportunity.

Jim scratched his head. "I don't know. There might be some in the supply box..." His voice trailed off uncertainly.

"Look, Jim, why don't you go back to work and I'll take care of Cal's hand. Rose has everything I'll need in her first-aid box and I know you must be busy."

It was almost too easy. Jim's brow raised and he said, "Gee, thanks. It would save me some time. The cut is near the base of his thumb and he really can't bandage it himself."

"Consider it done. I'll go right now," Lara said, heading for the cabinet under the sink where Rose kept the box.

"Good. See you later, Lara." Jim's footsteps had barely faded before Lara followed him down the back steps with the first-aid kit in her hand.

She was humming as she crossed the open field where she saw two hands exercising a stallion in the paddock, and still humming as she climbed the exterior staircase to Cal's loft. The door was ajar; she tapped on it and then pushed it open all the way.

Cal was sitting in the room's single easy chair, his shirt off and discarded on the bed, his hand bandaged clumsily with a towel.

He leapt to his feet when he saw Lara, then glanced behind her for Jim.

''What are you doing here?'' he asked her.

''Jim came to the house looking for disinfectant. I told him I'd help you, but if I had anticipated this kind of reception I would have let you bleed to death,'' Lara replied, stung. She kicked the door shut and advanced toward him, the first-aid box under her arm.

He had the grace to look abashed. ''I'm sorry. I was expecting Jim.''

''I regret disappointing you,'' Lara said crisply. ''I promise to get this over with quickly and not take up too much of your valuable time.'' She opened the kit briskly and added, ''Sit down, please.''

He obeyed, stretching his long legs in front of him and forcing her to move to his side.

''It's like an oven in here,'' Lara said, removing the sodden towel and examining the cut. ''Don't you ever use that thing?'' she asked, pointing to the ancient, battered air conditioner sitting silently in the back window.

''It just runs up Rose's electric bill—those old

ones are very inefficient," he replied sullenly. "I usually leave it off."

"This looks lovely," Lara said with an expression of distaste, studying the jagged flesh, which was still seeping blood. "Did you wash it?"

"I ran it under the tap in the sink."

"Very sanitary. If you don't mind I'll flood it with this disinfectant." She uncapped the bottle and held his hand over the discarded towel. "It may hurt."

He winced but made no sound as the reddish fluid ran into and over the cut. Lara dried it with the clean cloth she had brought and then squeezed a line of antiseptic ointment over the wound.

"Looks like you've done this before," Cal said grudgingly, watching her.

"I work with kids—it comes with the territory." She wrapped a layer of gauze around his hand.

"Thanks a lot," he said dryly.

She tightened the gauze and then fastened it in place, pulling the tape taut so it held the dressing securely.

"There you go," Lara said briskly. She tossed the tape and gauze into the box and closed it. "Leave that on for a full day and then you can uncover it. Keep up with the betadine and the ointment." She turned to leave.

Cal put his hand on her arm. "Thanks," he said huskily.

"You're welcome." She pulled away.

"Don't leave."

Lara looked up at him, at the dark eyes boring

down into hers, and at his parted lips, which showed a glimpse of his teeth.

"Why should I stay?" she said. "You made it plain when you saw me that you don't want me here."

"I want you here," he said grimly. "I want you everywhere."

Lara was stunned into speechlessness.

"You can't tell me that you didn't know," he said quietly.

"But ever since the night Rose fainted you've been avoiding me as if I were carrying typhoid," she whispered, staring. "I came here to...to..." She stopped.

"To what?" he murmured. He was still holding her arm, his body very close to hers in the small room.

"To see you," she finally said helplessly. "Just to see you at a distance of closer than twenty feet and talk to you without my grandmother listening to every word we said. For some reason that was important to me." Humiliated by the admission, she wrenched her arm from his grasp and bolted for the door.

Cal took one long step in front of her and blocked her path. She came up against his naked torso.

"Let me go," she said helplessly, beating her hands against his chest, near tears.

"I can't," he muttered huskily, pulling her into his arms. "I know I should, but I can't."

His mouth came down on hers so swiftly that Lara was immobilized, both by the sudden sweetness of the kiss and the power of his embrace. His mouth was surprisingly soft, parting hers with the skill of long practice. She lay back against his shoulder, luxuriating in the feel of hard muscles covered by satiny, sun-kissed skin, warm and supple against her bare arms. She ran her hands down his naked back, and he drew her closer as she caressed him, bending his head to bury his face in the fragrant mass of golden hair spread against her neck. When his mouth returned to hers he backed up, still kissing her, pulling her down onto the bed with him. She went willingly, gasping as she felt him hard and ready against her. As he twined his limbs with hers, imprisoning her beneath him, there was a knock at Cal's door.

They both froze.

Cal pulled away from Lara and sat up, breathing deeply, controlling himself with an effort. He didn't look at her.

"Yeah?" he finally said, clearing his throat.

"Cal, is Lara still in there? Bob Trask is down at the house looking for her," Jim replied.

Lara's heart sank at the change in Cal's expression. His face went blank and he said to Lara, "You heard the man. Trask is calling, you'd better run."

She stood up, arranging her clothing and smoothing her hair.

"Is that all you have to say to me?" she asked shakily.

He shrugged. "I wouldn't dream of keeping you from your boyfriend."

Lara picked up his shirt from the foot of the bed

and threw it in his face. Then she marched past him purposefully and yanked open the door.

"I'm on my way, Jim," she said. "Thanks for bringing me the message."

Jim looked in at Cal, who was standing, watching Lara depart. Something hung in the air, like the scent of ozone after a lightning strike. The foreman stared at Cal, then shrugged and followed Lara down the stairs.

Cal slammed the door smartly behind them.

Lara marched back to the house through the shimmering heat, dodging the gnats swirling around her head, nodding glacially to the hands who greeted her as she passed. Bob was in the kitchen with Rose, making small talk.

"Hi, Lara," he said brightly, smiling as Lara entered the room. "I was out this way on a call and I thought I'd stop in and give Rose that property map she asked me for last time I was here."

Lara managed to smile back, but her face still felt frozen. She wanted to kill Bob for just dropping by without calling—his timing could certainly use some work.

"How thoughtful," Lara said pleasantly. "Can I offer you a drink, or maybe a sandwich?"

"I already tried," Rose said, rising from her seat. "He's not biting. I'll be in the den, Lara. My last show is on now."

"I have to go, too," Bob said quickly, clearly uncomfortable with Rose's hasty, and obvious, retreat. "I just wanted to remind you to bring your swimsuit on Friday night. The department is renting out the

Sadler Country Club and the pool will be available to the guests."

Lara nodded.

"Well, duty calls," he said, sighing as he stood. He leaned over to peck Lara on the cheek. "I'll see you around seven on Friday."

"Okay, Bob. Thanks for stopping by."

Lara watched him go, then brought Rose a glass of juice.

"Nice guy," Rose observed, as Lara handed it to her.

Lara waited, expecting more, but Rose went back to her TV program.

Lara went back to her business books.

Rose managed to reserve comment on Bob's visit until they were preparing dinner that evening.

"You have a date with Bob Friday night?" Rose asked innocently, slicing a tomato.

"Yes."

Rose shook her head disapprovingly.

"What is that supposed to mean?" Lara demanded irritably.

"It means that you have no business leading that poor boy on this way. You have no more intention of getting serious with him than I have of flying to the moon. You're using Bob to avoid dealing with him," Rose said, nodding toward the screen door, through which Cal could be glimpsed digging a post-hole for the new bird feeder.

"I don't know what you're talking about," Lara said crisply, shaking off the bunch of lettuce that was in her hand and dropping it into the salad bowl.

"Oh, please, Lara Marie. Don't give me that look—I first saw it when I was changing your diapers. Do you think I haven't noticed the charge in the air around here? It feels like an electrical storm at dinner every night."

"Rose, the man barely speaks to me," Lara said, now avoiding her grandmother's eyes.

Rose snorted. "He wants to do a lot more than speak to you," she said shortly.

Lara could feel herself coloring, but she said nothing.

"Well?" Rose prompted.

"Stop badgering me! What am I *supposed* to do? We don't know a thing about him, Rose. He evades all questions about his past. We don't know who he is or where he came from, and that tells me he has something to hide."

"What does your heart tell you?"

Lara stared at her, bewildered.

"Cal has worked here for almost three months," Rose said. "In that time he has never complained, never shirked a task, put in a lot of overtime for which he has not been paid and never asked for a day off. And when I passed out on the floor in this very kitchen, what did he do? Did he walk away, or waste time calling an ambulance to get someone else to deal with the problem, or dial 911 and wait to see if somebody eventually turned up from Sadler? No, he picked me up, loaded me into the pickup truck and drove me to the hospital himself. Then he stood around until you showed up to make sure my prob-

had nothing when I married him, and for almost fifty years he was the best company I ever knew."

"Rose, aren't you jumping the gun a little?" Lara asked gently. "Cal hasn't exactly been offering me tons of encouragement."

"I'm sure he would like to, but can't you see his dilemma? He has a menial job here and, as everyone knows, you're the future owner of this place. The whole situation puts him in an awkward position. Not to mention your sham romance with Bob Trask, who from Cal's point of view must seem like a much more suitable candidate for your hand than himself."

"My hand? What is this, Rose, a Victorian novel?"

"You know exactly what I mean. I'm not going to beat this to death, Lara, but I want you to think about what I've said. Will you do that?"

"Yes," Lara replied quietly.

"Good. Now let's change the subject before I get maudlin. Did Jim say if he was able to get that dressage teacher to come in from Murphysburg?"

Lara answered, allowing the conversation to turn to the business of the ranch, but Rose's words haunted her, not only that night but all through her date with Bob. She realized that it made her uncomfortable to be identified as his girl by his friends and co-workers, something that was happening more frequently as the summer weeks passed. She really couldn't let the situation drift much longer.

Rose was right. It was not fair to Bob.

And her grandmother was right about something else. She *was* using Bob to deflect her attention from

Cal, and being forced to acknowledge that depressed Lara. She had never thought of herself as a moral coward, but this situation was bringing out behavior she had never previously exhibited, and didn't like.

When Bob dropped her off at home after the sheriff's department dance, she stood for several minutes in the yard, watching hundreds of fireflies dart about, lighting up the night. Crickets sent up a loud chorus and the cicadas in the bushes were deafening. Out at the pond a loon called plaintively, and a thin sliver of a moon hung in a starless, cloudy sky.

"How come you never ask your skinny friend into the house for a drink?"

The deep voice came booming out of the darkness, causing Lara to jump. She whirled to see the pinpoint light of a cigarette moving in the black night. She peered closer and saw Cal sitting on the side porch swing, one ankle crossed over the other knee, his left arm draped over the back of the chair.

"Have you been spying on me?" she demanded, outraged.

"Not at all. I was out taking a walk and stopped here for a smoke just before Trask turned into the driveway. Should I have run away?"

"You smoke too much," Lara said irritably, unable to refute the logic of his reply.

"You didn't answer my question."

"You can run away anytime you like," Lara said grimly.

"Not that question. Isn't it just good manners to invite your date inside for a nightcap?"

"Not that it's any of your business, but I'm tired..."

"And bored," he said.

"And there's no privacy in the house with Rose around," Lara finished, ignoring his interruption.

"Rose is asleep."

"She gets up every two hours, the medicine she takes contains a diuretic—" Lara stopped short as her eyes adjusted to the light and she saw that he was smiling.

"Why am I explaining myself to you?" she demanded furiously. "Scurry back to your sweatbox and sweat. I'm going to bed." She turned her back on him.

"Alone," he said, rising and walking toward her, tossing away his cigarette. "I'll bet Trask would like to change that."

"You shouldn't make nasty remarks about Bob. He talked Jerry Perkins out of suing you when Jerry woke up in jail with a dislocated jaw."

"I don't need that uniformed pretty boy to fight my battles for me," Cal said tersely. "Has he popped the question yet? I'll bet he has the ring picked out already."

"I'm not going to discuss him with you."

"Why not? Aren't you proud of your charming little romance? Isn't Trask quite the local catch—hometown boy, steady job with room for advancement, excellent career prospects?" He grabbed her arm and spun her around to face him, barely controlled fury in his tone. "It doesn't matter, does it, that he puts you to sleep and you can barely stand to have him touch you."

"How dare you say that to me?" Lara gasped, trying to pull away from him. "You have no right..."

"I have the right," he murmured, drawing her in close to him. "This gives me the right..." His mouth came down on hers so forcefully that Lara was at first stunned, then resistant, then pliant as he pressed her back against the wall of the house, covering her with his body. Her lips parted and she tasted his tongue, the tang of tobacco on his lips, the smooth hardness of his teeth. She whimpered as he lowered his hands to her hips and pulled her closer, letting her feel his arousal. He ducked his head and drew his mouth along the satiny line of her bare shoulder. Lara clutched him involuntarily, sagging helplessly in his grasp.

He kissed her for endless, tantalizing moments, then scooped her into his arms and carried her to a patch of grass, already damp with dew. He lowered her to the ground and then joined her immediately, unhooking the strap of her halter top and baring her breasts, taking a rigid nipple into his mouth.

Lara groaned and closed her eyes. She could barely breathe, the hot sensation of his mouth on her flesh became the center of her universe. When he lifted his head she whimpered at her deprivation.

"I hate the idea of his hands on you," Cal gasped. "When you're out with him I can't stop thinking about it."

She sighed as he ran his callused palm up her bare

leg, then bent his head again and sought her mouth eagerly.

"Why do you waste your time with him?" Cal demanded, moving his mouth to her cheek, her ear.

"You don't understand, you don't know..." Lara moaned incoherently, so awash in sensual lassitude that she was unable to articulate her feelings.

"I know when a woman wants me," Cal replied, his mouth traveling back to her breasts.

A woman? Lara thought, a painful notion penetrating her haze of desire. Is that how he saw her? Just a woman, any woman available to scratch an itch, satisfy a transitory urge? Indignation penetrated her fog of longing and she sat up suddenly, tearing herself away from Cal violently.

He stared at her, too far gone himself to immediately comprehend her change of mood.

Lara wanted to hurt him back, and she scrambled wildly for something to say that would wound him equally.

"If you know so much, what are you doing living in a room above a stable and working as a handyman for seven bucks an hour?" she demanded cruelly.

Lara saw the shaft sink home. His face went carefully blank and he released her instantly, completely, standing abruptly and turning his back on her.

Lara was silent, overwhelmed by what she had done. She had broken his terrifying spell over her and saved herself from an immediate mistake. But at what cost?

He looked back at her once, his dark gaze unreadable, then left, walking across the dew-laden grass until his shadow blended with the dark.

Lara refastened her halter with trembling fingers and then covered her mouth as if to call back the hurtful comment. But she was too late. The damage was done.

Lara stood, closing her eyes against tears, wishing she could take back the cutting words. How could she have been so unkind? Her resentment against Cal's indifference, whether real or feigned, must have been greater than she realized. She so desperately wanted him to step forward and stake his claim that his steadfast refusal to do it had been eating away inside her until it provoked this explosion. She had hit him where he was most vulnerable, and she wasn't proud of it.

She knew he would never speak to her again.

And he didn't. For the next week Cal looked through Lara as if she were a pane of glass. She took to riding Goldenrod every day, trying to wear herself out so she could sleep, but the tactic seldom worked. She woke at four every morning, wired as if about to take an exam, and prowled the house, checking on Rose, making several pots of coffee, riffling through magazines and going over account receipts for the business that she had already reviewed twice.

She was undone.

Lara had always believed, along with Blanche DuBois, that deliberate cruelty was not forgivable, so she couldn't excuse what she had said to Cal. Even if he did think of her as a passing distraction, her response was so viciously atypical that she was disgusted with herself. She was turning into someone she did not like: a frustrated, unhappy woman.

On a Monday morning following a weekend she had spent at the ranch, canceling her date with Bob after an attack of conscience, she rose at 4:15 and took a shower. While she made coffee in the kitchen she decided to saddle Goldenrod and go for a ride to catch the breeze that came, if at all, before dawn on a broiling July day.

There was just a hint of light in the sky as she left the house and walked to the stable. Goldenrod stamped in greeting, happy to see her a little earlier than usual, and Lara tried not to think of Cal sleeping in the loft above her as she readied the mare and led her outside.

It was still cool. The dewy grass clung to the horse's hooves as she followed the path to the pond, sure of the way she had gone many times before with different riders. Lara was easing up on the reins to let the horse take a drink when she realized that she was not the only early riser on the ranch.

Cal was swimming in the pond, cutting through the water in long, lazy strokes, his black hair plastered to his head, as sleek as a seal. Lara pulled back on the bridle to stop the horse, who seemed nonplussed and began to crop the sodden grass. Feeling like a voyeur, Lara watched as Cal finally emerged from the water and sprawled full-length on a towel, pushing back his hair with his hands and looking around lazily at the reddening sky.

His body was beautiful; each muscle was defined

and there was not an ounce of spare flesh anywhere. Her gaze lingered on the broad shoulders and well-developed arms, the long, slim legs, the ridges at the tops of his thighs, the pelt of black hair that narrowed to a thin line below his waist. He was beautiful, like a statue, a testament to the aesthetic benefits of physical labor.

Lara tore her gaze away. Her grandmother was right: she could not ignore what was happening with Cal. The very sight of him aroused emotions too powerful to dismiss. And her shame at hurting him was so great, her desire to comfort him so strong, that she wanted to leap down from the horse, run across the open field and fling herself into his arms.

But instead she turned the horse back into the trees and left the clearing. She couldn't go to him; they would doubtless just have another fight that would leave them both miserable, and still alone. If Cal couldn't open up, give of himself, commit in any way other than sexually, she couldn't force him to do it.

They had reached an impasse.

Lara cantered back to the house as the sun rose behind her.

Cal dozed off for a few minutes at sunrise; he woke with a start and glanced quickly at the watch he had set on top of his discarded clothes.

He sighed and relaxed. He still had plenty of time before he had to report to Jim Stampley for the day's roster of chores. He sat up and stared into the water, his elbows propped on his knees.

This was his last week at El Cielo. He hadn't told anyone yet, but he had made up his mind to go. He was obsessed with the girl and that was more than just dangerous, it was folly. He was making an idiot of himself, hanging around to watch her come home from dates as if they were both in high school, tormented by visions of her in another man's arms. And Lara was understandably bewildered by his contradictory behavior: keeping her at an emotional distance when he was clearly mad with desire for her. She was confused, suffering, and he knew he could never explain his actions.

It would be easier on her if he just left. But not easier on him. The idea of leaving her was like a physical pain, but one he would have to endure.

His circumstances left him with no other choice.

He blinked rapidly, pressing his thumb and forefinger against his eyes, feeling the pull of the healing cut Lara had bandaged against his palm.

Then he rose to dress. It was time to go to work.

Lara returned the horse to the stable and then went back to the house. As she passed Rose's bedroom she noticed that her grandmother's pillow had fallen to the floor. She went inside to pick it up, and as she lifted it onto the bed she saw that Rose's eyes were only half closed, her pupils set and staring.

Lara grabbed Rose's hand and found it stiff and cold.

Rose was dead.

Four

The days between Rose's death and her funeral passed in a haze of pain. Afterward Lara could barely remember individual events, which ran together in her mind like a child's watercolor; she had a general impression of calling people and planning the service, picking out the outfit Rose was to wear in the casket, talking to the rector at the church. And always Cal was there, lending quiet support, somehow sensing what had to be done and doing it before Lara could even ask, her prior harsh words to him seemingly forgotten. Don't get used to it, she warned herself. Don't rely on him. But she did anyway, too drained and grieving to worry about the future when the present was so bad.

It wasn't until everyone was gone, when Rose's bridge group had left and her church choir had deposited their baked goods and the rector had said his comforting speech and drove off with them, that Lara realized she was now alone at the ranch with Cal. She sat at the kitchen table and looked at the pile of mail, mostly sympathy cards she didn't want to answer, and the assortment of covered dishes, containing food she did not want to eat. The house was sickeningly, echoingly empty without Rose, who had lived in it for thirty years. The ticking of the clock over the sink sounded in Lara's ears as if it were the clanging of a gong.

She put her head down on her arms and cried.

She had known that Rose was failing, and of course Rose had known it, too, but Lara didn't realize until Rose was gone that she hadn't accepted it emotionally. Even Dr. Ponter's somber face the last time he examined her grandmother hadn't completely convinced Lara that the end was near. He had talked gravely about a lack of oxygen causing Rose's memory failure and waxen pallor and the blue tinge to her fingernails, but Lara hadn't really heard him because she didn't *want* to hear him. Rose's fainting spell had signaled the beginning of a fatal decline, but Lara's denial was so complete that it made her grief that much deeper.

It was several minutes before Lara realized that she had company. She looked up to find Cal standing in the doorway, propping the screen door open with his palm.

"Come in," she whispered, wiping her cheeks with the back of her hand.

He entered and stood uncertainly at her side, looking down, his dark gaze locked with hers.

"I want to thank you for everything you did to help me during the past few days," Lara said.

He nodded.

"It was good of you to overlook what I said to you—" she began, and he raised his hand.

"What you said was true," he interjected, shrugging.

"That doesn't excuse my rudeness," she said, and started to cry again.

He sat across from her and took her hand, waiting for the storm of weeping to pass. When it finally did Lara said, "I'm glad you came in to talk to me. Rose's lawyer contacted me this morning, and it looks like I'm going to sell this place."

Cal nodded again.

"I wouldn't be making this decision so quickly, but there are debts to be settled, and Jim Stampley has already told me that he won't be staying on past September. He has wanted to buy a smaller place of his own for a while...he was just waiting until Rose..." Lara put her fingers to her mouth and couldn't continue.

Cal's grip tightened.

She swallowed hard and said, "So with Jim gone and the creditors lining up to be paid, I don't have much of a choice. I don't know anything about training horses, I couldn't begin to find a replacement for Jim and the lawyer knows a real estate agent who might have a couple of interested buyers."

"I understand."

"It's just that I think Rose would have wanted me to keep El Cielo," Lara said softly. "She put so much of herself into this place, it seems a shame to see it go to strangers."

Cal said nothing.

"Will you stay until I find a buyer?" Lara asked him, too needy to be proud.

He hesitated briefly, then said, "Sure."

"Thanks."

Cal opened his mouth to say something else just as the doorbell rang.

Lara glanced up at the clock. "Oh, God, that's the real estate agent. I forgot he was coming," she said. "I have to let him in." She ran into the hall and pulled open the front door, glancing back into the kitchen as she did so.

Cal was already gone.

July became August, and the withering heat continued. A steady stream of people came to inspect El Cielo. Lara's life became a round of real estate agents and horse breeders and curious prospective buyers who poked into every cubbyhole of the house and outbuildings, taking notes. Lara listed the ranch at below market price in an attempt to sell it quickly, a tactic that brought out the bargain hunters. The agent received so many low offers that Lara finally gave him a basement figure and told him not to contact her unless he had a bid above it. That cut down on the calls but got her no closer to making a deal.

Lara was so lonely she took to telephoning her friends back in Chicago, an approach that would undoubtedly increase her monthly bill but didn't solve her problems. Cal worked steadily around the place, but he no longer came to dinner; once Rose died he told Lara she wasn't obligated to go on with that arrangement. He obviously wanted to avoid the intimacy that continuing the shared meals would provide, so Lara didn't reply that she would have roasted a fatted calf every night just to see him for one hour alone.

Lara had avoided Bob Trask since Rose's death, but about three weeks after the funeral she agreed to meet him for lunch in Red Springs. She had to be in town to see Rose's lawyer anyway, and she was so depressed about her relationship—or lack of one—with Cal that she accepted Bob's invitation. She wanted a change from listening for Cal's footfall or the sound of his voice, and from looking for him everywhere. A few hours away from the ranch, where she didn't anticipate coming upon him around every corner, might do her good. As she drove off in her compact she saw Cal working out by the road. He glanced up from the mailbox stand he was setting in a circle of wet cement to gaze after her departing car.

It was the closest he had come to meeting her eyes in about ten days.

The appointment with Rose's lawyer took a little longer than Lara had anticipated, and Bob was waiting for her in the aptly named Red Springs Diner when she arrived. He smiled when she slid into the booth across from him.

"Hi. I've missed you," he said.

"That's nice to hear. I've been busy. There's so much to do with settling the estate and putting the place up for sale." Lara picked up the menu and scanned the list of typed items, arranged on two sheets enclosed in a clear plastic folder.

"Is that the only reason you've been dodging me?" Bob asked, his gaze direct and challenging.

Lara looked up at him.

"I've seen you once since Rose died. At her wake."

"I just explained that. I'm sorry, Bob, but I haven't exactly felt like socializing."

Bob dropped the subject while the waitress took their order and then said, as the woman walked away, "I thought it might have something to do with your hired man."

Lara stopped fiddling with her purse strap. "Cal?" she said cautiously.

"Yeah. You seemed pretty chummy with him during the funeral service."

"He was helping me, Bob. He was fond of Rose, too."

The waitress brought two glasses of iced tea, and Lara waited until she had deposited them and left before adding, "What are you getting at, Bob?"

Bob sighed heavily. "There's been some talk. About you and Cal Winston."

Lara stared at him.

He shrugged. "You're living together out at the ranch, alone. Of course tongues will wag."

"We're hardly living together. I'm at the house and he has the loft above the stable."

"The point is that you're staying out there on an isolated spread with a man nobody knows, a man who just blew into town several months ago."

"And you've been appointed the public guardian of morals whose mission it is to discuss this with me?" Lara demanded tartly.

Bob colored slightly. "I'm concerned, Lara. It was clear at the funeral that the two of you have become...friendly. I'm not the only one who noticed that, and since this guy is a mystery man we're all worried about you."

"All? Who is 'all'?"

"Rose's minister mentioned it to me."

"Calvin Leach? Are you sure you didn't mention it to him?"

"We discussed it, let's put it that way," Bob said tersely.

"Who else?"

"Helen Kingston."

"Rose's bridge partner?" Lara started to laugh. "Don't you think you're reaching a bit with that one?"

The waitress deposited a salad in front of Lara and a hamburger in front of Bob.

"Anything else for you folks?" she said.

"We're fine," Bob replied. Then he leaned across the table as the waitress walked away. "Mrs. Kingston is extremely concerned about you," he said and picked up his burger.

"I just spoke to Helen on the phone last night and I'm going to visit her on Saturday morning at her son's house. She managed to control her extreme concern while she was telling me about her granddaughter's birthday party,'' Lara said dryly.

Bob put his hamburger down. ''Are you suggesting I'm lying to you?'' he demanded.

''I'm suggesting that you may be exaggerating the degree of gossip on this subject because...'' She stopped.

''Why?'' Bob said. ''Because I'm jealous of your Mr. Fixit?''

''I didn't say that.''

''But you were thinking it. Everyone else is thinking it, too. I was like the doorman at the funeral while you did everything and went everywhere with that drifter.''

It slowly dawned on Lara that her behavior had embarrassed Bob. He must have been leading the entire population of Red Springs to believe that he was getting serious with Rose's granddaughter, and then Lara had ignored him at the funeral in favor of the hired help. She had been too distracted to even think about it at the time, but now she realized that she had unwittingly made a fool of Bob in front of the guests at the wake, and word of it had gotten around town fast.

''I'm sorry if you feel I slighted you, Bob, but I never made you any promises,'' Lara said. ''I'm just surprised that it took you several weeks to tell me this.''

''I didn't think it was appropriate to bring it up when Rose had just died,'' he said.

''Oh, I see. You were waiting until my grief had

passed?'' Lara stabbed a piece of lettuce, then forked a cherry tomato.

He stared at her. ''You don't seem to realize that you're in a very precarious position. You're an heiress now and this guy might be after the ranch.''

Lara choked on a cucumber slice. ''Bob, please. Inheriting El Cielo makes me the owner of a heavily mortgaged property operating at a near loss, not an heiress.''

''You now own it, don't you? It's worth something, and in the right hands it could be managed and developed and someday be worth a lot more. By contrast, Cal Winston appears to own nothing more than the shirt on his back.''

''And you're suggesting that he has psychic powers? He decided to work at El Cielo because he somehow knew that Rose was going to die, and also knew in advance that I would show up at the right moment to inherit the place? I think you're giving him far too much credit.''

''I'm giving him credit for sizing up the situation as it stands now and realizing that landing Miss Lara Daniels could be to his extreme financial benefit.''

''The same could be said of you,'' Lara replied mildly, holding his gaze.

''I don't deserve that,'' Bob said, his eyes narrowing, his lips tightening into a white line.

''Neither does Cal.''

''How can you say such a thing? You don't even know him! No one does. He materialized here one day like a tumbleweed and wormed his way into the affections of a lonely old lady. Instead of resenting him for that you seem likely to keep on with Rose's foolishness."

"Rose was anything but a fool, and I'm a grown woman," Lara said, putting down her fork. "I can make my own decisions. I'm sorry if I'm not falling in with the plan you devised for the two of us, but a little gossip, even if it does exist, is not going to change my mind about a man who has done nothing but help me and my family. Thanks for the lunch, Bob. Goodbye."

Lara stood and turned quickly, heading down the aisle and out the door before Bob could stop her.

But Bob, who remained seated and watched her departure with a grim stare, had no intention of chasing her. He did, however, plan to look into the past life and habits of a certain Cal Winston.

As soon as possible.

Lara drove back to El Cielo in an agitated state, wondering why she had come so briskly to Cal's defense when she had the same questions about him that Bob did. It was one thing to dismiss Bob's concerns but another to dismiss her own; she was not as convinced of Cal's stainless background as she had made it sound. She knew that Bob had a point, and that made her even more eager to get away from him.

But it seemed that no amount of logic could affect how she felt about Cal. Her emotions were maddeningly impervious to reasonable argument. Was this infatuation, she worried as she turned into the driveway leading to the ranch, the downfall of so many impulsive lovers? Was she blinded by broad shoulders and a full mouth and soulful brown eyes?

Maybe so, but that didn't change anything. She was still dying for a word or a glance from Cal and he was still staying far away from her.

Lara's old guest, insomnia, moved in that night and seemed likely to stay for the duration. Instead of waking at four she now couldn't get to sleep at all. She began riding Goldenrod more often and even working out on a treadmill she had ordered. The result was extreme fatigue and a noticeable weight loss, but no additional sleep. She thought of contacting Rose's doctor for some pills, but was afraid that if she started taking them she would never stop. She thought of going back to Chicago and just letting the agent handle the sale of the ranch, but felt an obligation to select the buyer personally and see that everything was done as Rose would have wished. She thought, in fact, of many things, but was still watching Myrna Loy movies at 3:00 a.m. and eating tuna from a can for dinner every night.

One night in mid-August, when she had fallen asleep for an hour and then awakened again in a hyperconscious state, as if shot with adrenaline, she abandoned her bed in disgust. Dressing in jeans and a T-shirt, Lara walked down to the stable, intending to saddle Goldenrod for a night ride. What did it matter if she prowled the property on horseback in the wee hours? She owned the place, and there was nobody around but Cal, who was asleep.

The moon was almost full and the night exceptionally still as she entered the stable. The heat had rendered everything comatose, except for Lara, of course, and a few persistent crickets. Goldenrod pricked up her ears when she saw Lara, but then backed away when Lara approached her with the saddle.

What's the matter? Lara wondered. Does the horse know what time it is? She tried again, and this time, the horse kicked wildly, whinnying loudly. Alarmed, Lara retreated, then slipped on the straw and fell against the wall of the mare's stall. Trapped, she watched in terror as the horse bucked and whinnied, kicking the walls until wood chips flew. Lara cowered motionlessly, afraid to move, afraid to breathe. She didn't know what was wrong but was too frightened to investigate. Everything seemed to be happening in slow motion; the horse's fit seemed to go on forever.

Lara was just considering trying to crawl out of the way when she heard a sound to her left. She turned her head and saw Cal, dressed only in a pair of jeans, watching the scene from the door. She looked on anxiously as he came closer and she called, "Cal, stay back."

He ignored her, creeping nearer and then running into the stall and reaching for the horse's bridle.

"Go!" he shouted to Lara, who scrambled to her feet as he tried to control the bucking horse. She flattened herself against the wall, inching past him as he struggled with the animal, then bolted to safety when he got Goldenrod to respond. She watched, panting, as he gradually calmed the horse, making soothing noises and gesturing with his free hand for Lara to move even further away.

Once Goldenrod was settled Lara noticed something she should have seen before, that the horse was favoring her left forefoot. Cal saw it, too, and Lara's eyes widened as he fell to his knees and lifted the hoof, examining its underside.

Amazingly the horse let him do it, and Lara watched as he reached into his pocket and extracted a penknife. Slowly, carefully, he pried a sizable stone loose from the shoe and tossed it into the straw on the floor of the stall. Then he released the mare's leg, and she gingerly set it on the ground, testing for soundness. Once she felt that the offending object had been removed, she bent her head and began leisurely munching hay from two bales stacked in the corner.

Lara's heart was pounding so hard she felt she should be able to hear it. She watched as Cal backed out of the stall slowly, then turned to face her.

Everything she felt was in her eyes. He opened his arms and she ran into them.

"What the hell are you doing here at this hour?" he said into her ear, as she clung to him and sobbed.

"I couldn't sleep. I thought I'd take a ride...I didn't see that she was lame."

Cal held Lara off to look at her. "She just didn't want you to mount her and make the pain worse with your weight."

"I didn't realize you knew so much about horses," Lara said, looking up at him through her tears.

"I've learned. I've been watching the hands work them, and I come in and visit them sometimes. I could see right away that Goldenrod had something in her shoe.''

''I should have noticed. I've just been so tired...'' Lara began, and then started to cry again.

''All right, all right,'' he said soothingly. ''It doesn't matter, you weren't hurt and the horse is okay. I woke up when Goldenrod started whinnying, I thought the place was on fire.'' He ran his hands down Lara's back, and murmured, ''You're getting thinner, Lara. Don't you eat anything?''

''Not alone,'' she whispered. ''I'm always alone, Cal. Why am I always alone?''

''Oh, baby, I don't want you to be alone,'' he said in a broken voice. His lips found hers, and Lara kissed him back urgently, unable to pretend reluctance when she wanted him so much. He explored her mouth with his own as she clung to him, her fingers tracing the hard ridge of his spine. He lowered his mouth and drew it along the line of her collarbone, leaving a trail of heat and moisture on her skin. She sighed, closing her eyes tightly, swaying in his arms until he picked her up and set her carefully on a bed of straw, dropping next to her and rolling her closer to him in the same movement.

Lara arched her back as he grasped the hem of her shirt and pulled it up, his seeking hand cupping her breast, his thumb rasping the nipple until she whimpered and pressed it back into his palm. She sank her fingers into the wealth of hair at his nape as he bent and took the rigid peak into his mouth, shoving her shirt aside impatiently until he lost patience and sat up, yanking it over her head. She moaned as he embraced her again, her naked torso pressed to his superheated skin as he lowered her back to the ground and moved on top of her.

Lara shifted position, her legs opening instinctively, and he groaned helplessly at her implied submission, grinding his hips into hers. Lara felt him, stallion full against her thighs, and she turned her head to whisper into his ear, "Make love to me, Cal. I need you so much."

She felt him stiffen, and then he pulled away from her, sitting up abruptly and propping his elbows on his knees. His hands were shaking and his shoulders heaved with the force of his heavy breathing. He didn't look at her.

Lara lay on her bed of straw, bewildered, bereft. "Cal?" she said softly. "Cal, what is it?"

He didn't answer.

It was several seconds before she realized that he wasn't coming back to her. Then she sat up, stabbed around on the floor for her shirt, locating it blindly and pulling it on inside-out.

"I can't believe I fell for your act again," she muttered, rising unsteadily. "I must be the biggest simpleton on the face of the earth. Is this your payback for the night of the fireflies?"

"No," he said huskily, still not looking at her. "I don't expect you to understand, but please believe that isn't true."

"Believe you?" she said incredulously, her voice rising. "Why the hell should I believe you? Your sole occupation seems to be making a fool out of me. You stay away for weeks and let me pine for you, and then you give me hope, you make me want you..." She stopped, determined not to cry again, and he looked around at her finally, his expression tortured.

"I don't mean to do that," he said quietly. "But I can't take advantage of you this way. There's no future in it... I can't offer you anything..."

Lara wasn't listening, her outrage building and fueling her anger, which mercifully eclipsed her pain. She pulled off her shoe and threw it at him.

"Why do you always do this to me?" she screamed, as he ducked the flying missile. "I can't take it anymore—I can't eat, I can't sleep, I'm looking for you every minute of every day behind every tree. You are driving me to the brink of insanity! If you can't make up your mind, I'll do it for you. I want you off this place first thing in the morning. I don't care what you do or where you go. You can go straight to hell, just be out of here by nine. I don't want to see you again, is that clear? Do you understand me?"

He didn't answer, but his stony expression spoke volumes. Lara ran from the stable and sprinted back to the house, not stopping until she had slammed her bedroom door behind her. She tore off her clothes and stepped into the shower, letting the cool water wash the hot tears from her face and the odor of Cal's sweat from her body. She stayed in the shower a long time, then bundled herself into her oversize pajamas and walked slowly back to the kitchen, intending to get a cool drink and then go back to bed.

Cal was standing at the entrance to the front hall, wearing a suede jacket despite the heat, a zippered canvas bag at his feet.

Lara closed her eyes, too drained for another confrontation. "What are you doing here?" she said wearily.

"There's no reason for me to wait until morning. I thought it would be better to just go," he replied quietly.

"Oh, I understand. You want the money I owe you," she said insultingly.

"I'm paid up until yesterday," Cal said quietly. "Today's on the house."

"Thanks a lot," Lara said sarcastically.

He waited.

"So what *do* you want?"

"Before she died Rose said that she had left something for me in the top drawer of her dresser. I think she knew her time was limited and…" He stopped.

"Well?" Lara demanded testily, in no mood to hear again how fond her grandmother had been of this maddening man.

"Could you look for it?" he asked.

"Look for what?"

"Whatever it is Rose left me," he replied patiently, not rising to the bait of her irritated tone.

Lara stared at him balefully.

"I want it to remember her by after I'm gone," he added. "I never had any real family and I figure Rose is the closest I'm ever going to come to it, and—"

"I don't know what you're talking about," Lara said flatly, interrupting him. "I went through Rose's things after she died and gave her clothes to charity. I didn't see anything labeled for you, so please just go."

"Do you mind checking again?" he said quietly. "It would mean a lot to me. She said the top drawer of her dresser, specifically."

Lara sighed loudly but went down the hall to Rose's room. As she pulled open the drawer she suddenly remembered that the only thing left in it was Rose's well-worn, leather-bound Bible.

Lara picked it up and opened the book to the flyleaf, where she saw written in Rose's slightly shaky hand: "For Cal, who came into my life at the end of it and reminded me more of my late beloved husband than any other man I ever met. Godspeed."

Lara's vision blurred as she looked at the familiar handwriting, then she wiped her eyes and brought the book out to Cal, who looked up as she emerged from the bedroom.

"Here it is," Lara said softly. "You were right."

He took the book from her and stood looking down at the inscription so long that she finally said, "Cal?"

He didn't move. It was several more seconds before she saw that his lashes were wet and the muscles in his throat were working.

He was crying.

All the anger Lara had felt in the stable fled from her in a rush of sympathy. She put her hand on his arm and said, "Oh, Cal."

The Bible fell to the floor as he embraced her.

"I don't want to go," he said huskily, his mouth against her ear. "If you only knew how much I want to stay with you."

Five

Lara drew back to look up at him. "Then stay. For God's sake, Cal, I'm begging you."

He shook his head hopelessly, unable to speak.

"What is it, Cal? Can't you tell me?"

His grip tightened. "I won't draw you into it," he finally said grimly.

"Even if I want to be in it?" She stood on tiptoe to kiss him, and he responded wildly, almost desperately, conveying the need he was always hesitant to express in words.

"Can't I help you?" Lara said against his mouth. "Please, let me help you." She ran her hands down his arms and then up, inside the collar of his shirt.

He grasped her wrists and held her at arm's length, his breathing ragged, his expression rapt.

"Listen to me, Lara. I have to talk to you, and I can't do it when you're..."

"What?" she said innocently.

"Doing that," he murmured, closing his eyes as she leaned into him and kissed the hollow of his throat.

Lara stepped back and he released her.

"All right," she said. "I'm listening."

He took a deep breath. "I know you want to help me, but you have to take my word for it that no one can. You must accept that I have to go, or stay here on my terms with no questions asked."

Lara searched his face, but it was closed. "You drive a hard bargain," she said.

"It's the only way, Lara. It's the only way to make sure my trouble doesn't ruin your life, too. I've been selfish enough to get involved with you when I knew I shouldn't, but I won't go further than that. I should have run in the other direction the day I met you, but I was too weak, or maybe just too lonely. The most important thing for you to understand now is that if you know nothing about me, you can't be accused of sheltering me. Your ignorance will protect you."

"Protect me from what?" she asked, impressed by the passionate intensity and the length of his speech. His taciturnity had suddenly vanished.

He shook his head again, then took her face between his hands and said, "Just tell me this. If we're together for only a little while, will it be worth it to you?" he asked huskily. "Can you live for today, take what we have now and not think about the future?"

Lara didn't hesitate. "Yes, yes. After waiting for so long I'll take what I can get."

"Then don't ask me any questions and you won't force me to lie to you," he said flatly.

"I need to ask you only one question," Lara said. "Do you love me?"

He pulled her close again and there was a long pause before he answered huskily, "I love you, Lara. I always have. No matter what happens, never doubt that for a moment."

Lara's eyes closed blissfully as his soft voice caressed her. She had thought she would never hear him say it.

"And you won't stop this time?" she whispered, as he pushed her loose top off her shoulders and sought the satiny skin of her shoulder with his mouth.

"I can't stop," he muttered, bending to slip an arm under her knees. "Not anymore." He swung her up into his arms and carried her into her darkened bedroom.

Lara lay back against the pillows as he stripped off his jacket, dropping it on the floor. He joined her on the bed and kissed her once more, his mouth hot, urgent, as if he would consume her. His beard stubble grazed her cheek as he undid the buttons of her top, drawing it away from her body and exposing her naked torso. When he reached for the light on her nightstand she stayed his hand.

"I want to see you," he murmured, bending to kiss her again.

"I'm shy," Lara whispered. "Please."

He withdrew his hand and pulled her into his arms.

"I'm sure the rest of you is just as beautiful as your breasts," he said. He lowered his head and buried his face between them, his strong fingers enclosing her waist, his mouth moving down to her navel, his tongue thrusting and tracing the depression in her flesh. Lara sighed and sank her fingers into his hair, holding his head against her. She could just see him in the shaft of light falling across her bed from the bathroom; his dark hair caught and reflected the yellow glow with a dull sheen. He turned and pressed his hot cheek to her abdomen, his lips parted, his eyes closed, the black lashes lacey against his tanned skin. He drew a deep breath and sighed luxuriously, as if this was where he had longed to be and had finally come home.

When he sat up Lara watched him move from the bed and strip off the rest of his clothes, a mobile shadow in the dim room. Then he lay down next to her, not touching her except for his hand tracing the line of her hip and leg. His rough palm contrasted with the silken smoothness of her calf as he said, "You have the loveliest legs."

"Skinny," she said, smiling.

"Oh, no." He bent and kissed her ankle, then her shin, then her knee. Suddenly he pulled her to him and stroked her bare back.

"Oh, Lara, I love you so much. It's such a relief to tell you, I've been carrying that knowledge around with me like a guilty secret for too long."

Lara felt her throat close with emotion as she put her arms around his neck and held him tightly, inhaling the now familiar fragrance of his skin, his hair.

She was so in love with him that she didn't care about anything but this man and this moment. When he began to kiss her again, demandingly, she responded in kind, moaning when he rolled her under him and she felt him completely, his bare body pressed to the length of hers for the first time. He stroked her breasts, coaxing her nipples into rigid peaks. Lara sighed, the sound growing deeper and more rapturous as his caresses intensifed. Then she gasped aloud as she felt the sudden heat of his mouth enclose a tender bud, then the light grazing of his teeth against it. His hand trailed down her body; she stiffened, then relaxed, as he slipped it under the waistband of her pants and the swell of sensation overcame her.

"Do you like that?" he whispered.

Lara arched toward him eagerly, unable to answer, seeking his touch. When he moved to pull off the pajama bottoms she lifted her hips to accommodate him. As the thin garment floated to the floor he bent and traced the line of her thigh with his tongue, leaving a trail of fire across her body. He teased her, kissing, licking, nipping her lightly every place but where she desired the contact.

"Please," she moaned, writhing restlessly on the bed.

"What?" he said hoarsely, as lost as she was. "What do you need?"

Lara opened her eyes and looked down at him. His tanned skin was dewed with a fine mist of sweat, and as she grasped his shoulders her fingers slid across the slick, muscular surface, then settled on his hair, damp and curling. He was absorbed in his exploration of her body, his hands gripping her hips, his whole frame tense and coiled, anticipating release.

As she watched, he bent suddenly and she felt his mouth where she had most wanted it. Her nails dug into his scalp and she squeezed her eyes shut again, helpless before an onrush of pleasure unlike anything she had previously experienced. The exquisite torture mounted, growing more and more intense, and she whimpered, finally crying out and trying to drag him upward.

"Now," she said, barely able to speak. "Please, now."

He slid along the bed to lie next to her and took her hand, placing it on him. He pulsed against her fingers, and he molded her to him as she touched him lightly, then more firmly. She felt her power as her touch caused him to gasp aloud and then finally roll away from her.

"What is it?" Lara said. "Did I hurt you?"

He shook his head, incapable of speech. He held out his arms and she went into them, feeling his muscles tense to receive her, the friction of his hair against her bare skin. For the first time she took the initiative, kissing his chest, the flat nipples nestled in dark hair, the line of hair that bisected his middle. She caressed the long, ropy muscles of his thighs and the firm, smooth surface of his abdomen. His eyes were slits as he watched her, holding her lightly, remaining passive until she enclosed him with her fingers once more. He then pulled her into a prone position and said huskily, "I need you now, Lara. I can't wait any longer." He dipped his hand between her legs and she arched against him, moaning helplessly as he found her ready. More than ready.

He stroked her thighs and they fell apart, welcoming him. He pulled her into position and thrust into her as she wrapped her legs around him.

Lara stiffened and cried out, pulling away from him. Cal withdrew in amazement, staring down at her.

"Oh, baby," Cal said softly, wonderingly, "why didn't you tell me?" He drew her back into his arms and rocked her tenderly.

Lara turned her head away from him, her eyes closing. "I was embarrassed, I thought you might be turned off, or scared off, or..." She stopped as a tear slid from under a sealed lid and down her cheek.

He didn't say anything for a long time, and when he did his voice sounded congested, barely under control. "If I had known it was your first time I would have been gentler, taken more time..." he said softly.

Lara buried her face against his chest. "You were perfect. It's me. I just couldn't find a way to tell you, and then it seemed like you would leave and this would never happen. But I guess it hasn't." She lay back against his shoulder, gazing up into his eyes. "Will it ever happen now?"

His answer was to set her back on the bed and begin to make love to her again. He moved slowly, carefully, forcing her to relax, leading her back to the brink until she was pulling him over her, urging him to try again. He did, and this time she followed where he led, losing herself in him completely.

And afterward when she lay dozing in the curve of his arms, her body singing with the new lesson it had learned, her gratification was complete.

Lara's life was transformed by the first night she spent with Cal in Rose's house. Once they became lovers they shared a secret that set them apart. During the day they were circumspect because of the presence of the hands, but once the workers went home they were like two kids let out of school. They had dinner together every evening in Rose's kitchen, then retired to the bedroom, where they spent long, leisurely hours making love and talking about everything—but not, of course, the forbidden topic of Cal's past. To Lara he seemed perfectly content, except in those odd moments when he didn't think she was watching him and she saw the shadow cross his face, reminding her that all was not as it seemed. What was the problem? she wondered. Had he robbed a bank, pilfered government secrets? Was he AWOL? Was he married? She knew she was enjoying fleeting happiness that could end at any moment, but for the most part Lara managed to brush the negative thoughts away and was happier than she would have thought possible.

One Saturday morning toward the end of August, as Cal was rinsing off at the pump and Lara was sitting on the back steps watching him, he suddenly said, "Let's go somewhere tonight. Somewhere nice. You never get away from this house."

Lara didn't answer. Unspoken between them was the agreement that they shouldn't flaunt their relationship in Red Springs. Their presence in town on a "date" would confirm suspicions that Lara would rather let lie.

"We could go to Murphysburg," Cal suggested. "There's a restaurant there everyone talks about, The Something Isle."

Lara considered that idea. Murphysburg was over an hour away, probably a safe distance.

"The Mystic Isle," Lara said. "I went there once years ago with my parents."

Cal nodded. "Why not?"

Lara grinned. "What would you wear?"

He glanced down at his jeans and the T-shirt lying on the ground. "Not this," he agreed.

"There's a men's store on the main street in Murphysburg. We could go early and get you something to wear."

"You're not buying me any clothes," he said darkly.

"Don't be ridiculous, Cal. Think of it as a cash advance on your salary. If you want to go to a place like that restaurant you have to dress properly."

He sighed as he yanked the T-shirt back over his head. "Oh, all right. I'll go in and make the dinner reservations. If we leave early enough we can stop off and get a sports jacket on the way."

"And slacks. No jeans," Lara said.

"All right. No jeans."

Lara swatted him with a towel as he walked past her, and he bent and snatched her up into his arms.

"Mmm, you smell good," Lara said, rubbing her nose on his sun-warmed, freshly washed shoulder.

"I feel good, too," he said huskily, taking her hand and running it up the inside of his leg.

"Yes, you do," Lara whispered, closing her eyes and pulling him tighter against her.

He picked her up and carried her into the bedroom, where they spent the rest of the day, rising only to eat lunch. When evening came Lara dressed in an ivory silk suit and high heeled sandals as Cal got her car. He returned and stood in the doorway as she put up her hair and added pearl earrings and a choker to her outfit.

"You are so beautiful," he said softly, as she picked up her purse and came toward him. "You could have anyone. What are you doing with me?"

"I love you," Lara replied, putting her head on his shoulder.

"I'm doing a very selfish thing in staying here," he said soberly, sinking his fingers into the collar of her jacket and rubbing her neck. "I know it, but I can't seem to stop myself."

Lara was silent.

Cal held her close for a few moments longer and then said, "We'd better get going."

Murphysburg was hardly New York, but it was about four times the size of Red Springs and boasted several fine restaurants, a movie theater and an honest to goodness shopping district. Cal was silent and looking less than thrilled as they entered Dunstall's, a boys and men's outfitter that had been in business for about fifty years. The middle-aged clerk surveyed

Cal with a practiced eye and produced half a dozen jackets instantly, all of which looked wonderful on him.

"That was fast," Lara said to the woman, who stood by as Cal tried on the last one.

"He's a perfect 42 long," the clerk replied, "not to mention that face. Anything is going to look like designer goods on him. My job should always be so easy. Where did you find him?"

"On my grandmother's ranch," Lara replied, smiling.

"Can you give me the address?" she asked. "My daughter is still single, and looking hard."

Lara laughed and went over to Cal, who was surveying himself critically in the three-way mirror.

"Let's take this and get it over with," he said darkly to Lara. "That woman thinks I'm your gigolo."

"Don't be silly. Couples shop together all the time." Lara studied him carefully. "I think I like the brown raw silk one better."

"Fine, whatever. I *feel* like your gigolo, dressing up like Casanova while you stand there watching me."

"How about a shirt and tie to go with that?" the clerk said behind them. "Fifteen and a half, thirty-five. Am I right?"

"Right," Cal said, looking at her.

The clerk strode off on her errand and Cal said to Lara, "Now I remember why I avoid these places. Nothing makes me feel stupider than standing around trying on clothes in front of a bunch of women."

"You'd never make a fashion model. And two women hardly constitute a bunch," Lara replied, grinning.

"What are they, telephone poles?" Cal said, gesturing at four teenage girls who were lingering at the tie counter, glancing at him covertly and then giggling wildly.

"They're just dumbstruck by your beauty," Lara said, batting her eyelashes.

"I'm leaving," Cal responded, and strode past her purposefully. He almost crashed into the returning clerk, who handed him a cream shirt and a beige-and-brown striped tie. He took them from her and fled to the changing room.

"He doesn't look happy," the clerk said to Lara, who rolled her eyes.

"I don't think he's worn a tie in a long time—he may be afraid it will cut off his circulation," Lara said. "Which reminds me, can you wrap up that other jacket, the navy one, and send it to me? I'd like to surprise him with it. It may be an ice age before I can get him into a store like this again."

"Sure thing," the clerk said, pleased at the double sale.

"Let me pay for it now so he won't know," Lara said, extracting her credit card from her purse.

"Where shall I send it?" the clerk asked, taking a sales slip from a drawer.

"El Cielo ranch in Red Springs," Lara replied, handing her the card. "Postal Route 3."

"Daniels?" the woman said, looking down at it. "You aren't Rose Daniels's granddaughter!"

"Yes, why?" Lara asked warily, feeling her stomach starting to sink. The woman's expression was too delighted, too avid.

"I'm Bob Trask's Aunt Maisie. I live next door to his parents in Sadler. Bob has been telling us all about you."

Lara tried to keep her dismay from showing on her face. "Oh, really? Well, it's nice to meet you."

"Weren't you dating Bob recently?" Maisie asked, as she processed the sale.

"Earlier in the summer, just casually," Lara replied, wishing that Cal would hurry up and return.

"I thought Bob mentioned that. I was sorry to hear about your grandmother. We all admired the way Rose hung on to that place through thick and thin." She paused meaningfully. "I hear you're trying to sell it now."

"That's right," Lara said grimly, wondering if the woman were mentally calculating how many sports jackets Lara could buy for her lover with the proceeds from the ranch.

"What a shame," Maisie said.

"My foreman is leaving and I really have no idea how to run it," Lara added.

Maisie nodded dolefully. "I guess it's not like the old days, when people kept property in the same family for generations." She folded the jacket and stowed it beneath the counter. "I'll send it out on Monday, the receipt will be in the box."

"Thank you."

Cal finally appeared, wearing the new clothes with his tan pants and loafers. He looked gorgeous, but

Lara was too distracted to appreciate the effect of their selections.

"You okay?" he said to Lara, sotto voce, as he took out his wallet and paid cash for his purchases.

"Why?"

"You look a little...green," he murmured.

"I'm fine."

Cal took his change from the clerk and said, "Thanks a lot."

"Enjoy your purchases. You look wonderful in them," Maisie replied. And then she added to Lara, "I'll be sure to say hello to Bob for you. I'll be seeing him tomorrow."

"Thanks," Lara said resignedly. "Goodbye."

"Bob who?" Cal asked as they walked down the aisle of the store.

Lara sighed. "Bob Trask. That lady was his aunt."

Cal stopped walking and looked down at her. "The cop?"

"Can you believe my luck?" Lara said glumly. "She's probably burning up the phone wires right now, describing our little shopping trip in the most colorful terms."

"You dumped him, didn't you?"

Lara nodded.

"Because of me?"

"Because of the way I felt about you. He was lecturing me about how the townspeople were gossiping, discussing in detail our illicit liaison out at the ranch."

"I see. That was before we got together?"

"Yes. It seems that the prevailing opinion among

the cognoscenti in Red Springs is that you are after the vast fortune I will acquire when I finally sell El Cielo."

"But you don't think that, do you?" he said quietly, watching her face.

"Cal, don't be absurd. I never saw a man resist a woman harder than you resisted me. If your plan was to seduce the incipient heiress then you were certainly going about it the wrong way."

"So why are you worried? If the woman wants to talk, let her talk. Let's go."

His tone was light, but Lara saw his expression as he held the door for her on the way out of the shop.

They went on to the restaurant, and after a glass of wine and a few hors d'oeurves Lara was able to cast off the pall of her meeting with Maisie Trask and enjoy herself. The food was excellent, and she discovered, not to her surprise, that Cal could handle plush surroundings as easily as he handled the ranch. They had a long, leisurely dinner, and when Cal led her onto the dance floor he said into her ear, "Remember this night, Lara. Remember how much I love you, and no matter what else happens, that won't change."

Lara stopped moving and looked up at him. "What do you mean? Cal, you're scaring me."

"Don't be scared, baby. Just hold this moment in your mind. Good memories help get you through the rough times, and this evening will make a good memory."

He pulled her closer, and Lara said nothing more, but his fatalistic tone was not lost on her. He certainly sounded as if the rough times were just around the corner.

Back at the house he made love to her as if she were a fragile vessel, a precious object to be preserved and revered. And afterward, Lara listened to his breathing slow down, then grow deep and even, and she said a little prayer, beseeching the heavens to let him stay with her.

Whatever the problem, it couldn't be stronger than her love for him.

Nothing was.

Cal was up before Lara the next morning, and after he showered in her pink-tiled bathroom he sat on the edge of the bed and watched her sleep. She was curled on one side, her lips parted, her pale hair cascading over one eye. He lifted a lock of it and ran it through his fingers, marveling at its corn-silk texture. Then he let the strands drop and pulled the sheet up to her shoulder, patting it into place. He stood again and went to the window, looking out across the field to the stable where he used to sleep.

He no longer knew if he had done the right thing when he decided to stay with Lara; he had ceased to think when he first made love to her and cast his lot with hers. Now he lived from day-to-day, savoring each moment, aware that each night he spent with her might be the last night. He didn't know how long this idyll could continue, but he would have the memory of it for the rest of his life. And so would Lara. Whatever pain their parting caused would be less than the pain he would have inflicted by leaving her before it began.

Lara stirred and he looked back at her. She sighed and settled down again, one arm flung across her pillow. Cal studied her sleek form, only partially concealed by the sheet, and felt the stirring in his gut that she had inspired from the very beginning.

He had never loved anyone so much; the thought of her disillusionment when she learned the truth about him made him want to pummel the walls with his fists. He knew he was greedy to take what he could, when he could, but it was what Lara wanted, too. He simply didn't have the strength to deny them both the satisfaction they found in each other's arms.

Lara rolled over and searched the empty bed with a seeking hand. Her eyes opened and she saw Cal standing across the room.

"Hi," he said.

She held out her arms.

He walked over to the bed and joined her, blotting out the uncertain future with the happy present.

"I missed you," Lara said drowsily.

"I missed you, too," he replied, kissing the side of her neck as he embraced her. "That's a new feeling for me."

"Missing somebody?" Lara said, looking up at him.

He nodded. "My style was never to get close enough to form attachments, so there was nobody to miss."

"What was it like to be so alone as a kid?" Lara

asked, wondering if he would deflect the question again.

He shrugged. "All the kids I lived with were alone, really, in the sense that we had no parents. The nuns were always kind, but you knew they were taking care of you because they loved God, not because they loved you. It makes a difference."

Lara nodded, trying not to picture him in some gray, institutional room with the single beds lined up in a row, as if they were an illustration in a children's book.

"So there were no beatings or starvation, no *Oliver Twist* or *Jane Eyre?*"

"Jane who?"

"Never mind. Were you mistreated?"

"No, they just treated everybody the same. And what you want is to be treated differently, specially, as if you are a unique person."

"You are," Lara said warmly, hugging him tighter. "Did it change after your foster parents took you in?"

"They were good people, but he was killed a year after they got me, and she couldn't go it alone, so I wound up back at St. Anne's. And you know how kids are...there was a lot of talk about me being tossed back into the pond, not making the grade. The others were jealous that I got selected for a home, since most never are, and kids can be cruel." He stroked her hair absently, seeing it all again. "What every child in that situation wants most is a family," he added quietly.

"You have me now," Lara said gently, trying to wipe out the memory of that pain.

For how long? Cal wondered, then pushed the thought away and drew her down to the bed.

Lara was dusting Rose's porcelain figurines in the living room a few days later when the first police car pulled up in front of the house. She didn't become alarmed until she saw that it was followed by two others, state vehicles by their medallions. The sheriff's sedan had its blue lights flashing, and her polishing cloth fell from her hand when she saw Bob Trask emerge from the car with his gun drawn. She ran to the door as he came running up the steps, his expression one of grim satisfaction.

"Where's Winston?" he said when he saw her emerge from the house. Behind him the other police officers were gathering, their eyes focused on Lara.

"He's out back with Jim Stampley," Lara said, her gaze moving from Bob to the others. "Why?"

Bob nodded and gestured for the rest of the cops to circle the house. "We're here to take him into custody."

"Custody?" Lara whispered.

"That's right. Your boyfriend is wanted in Connecticut. For murder."

Six

"Murder?" Lara whispered, unable to believe it. She of course had considered that Cal might be in trouble with the law, but murder? The very word was black, staggering, a plunge into the void. It had never even occurred to her, and it had to be a mistake.

Cal couldn't kill anyone.

"There must be some confusion about this," she said dazedly, searching Bob's face.

"I don't think the authorities in Hartford are confused," Bob replied crisply. "They've been looking for Winston for over a year. His real name is Caleb Churchill, and he's accused of killing a man during a fight."

"Then it was self-defense," Lara said, quickly seizing the exonerating explanation.

"The arresting officer didn't think so. I've read

his report, and it seems your friend is a Golden Gloves boxer whose hands are considered lethal weapons. He was charged with second-degree murder and escaped when he was being transferred from one facility to another by knocking out a guard."

Lara had a flash memory of Cal whirling to punch Jerry Perkins, saw again the lightning speed of the move and the pinpoint accuracy of the blow. She felt a falling sensation in the pit of her stomach as she realized that what Bob was saying must be true.

They both looked up as the state cops came around the corner of the house with Cal in tow. He was handcuffed with an officer on either side of him, each holding one of his arms, and two following behind him. Cal was walking slowly and staring at the ground.

"Any resistance?" Bob said to the state cop who was closer to Lara.

He shook his head as he ushered Cal past them.

"Can I talk to him?" Lara asked Bob.

"I don't think you understand the situation, Lara," Bob said flatly. "This man is now my prisoner, and will remain so until I turn him over to the Connecticut authorities." His tone was pompous, his attitude detached and official. He was enjoying his triumph.

"If he's your prisoner then you can give me permission to talk to him," Lara persisted.

Bob shook his head disgustedly. "Throw in the towel, Lara. He's a loser."

"Are you taking him to the Red Springs jail where we gave the incident report?" Lara asked, as if she hadn't heard him.

Bob sighed. "Yes."

"I'll be there right after you," she said, watching as one of the cops put his hand on the top of Cal's head and then shoved him into the rear seat of the police car. Just as he was vanishing inside the sedan Cal looked back over his shoulder at Lara, and her blood froze at the expression of utter resignation on his face.

It was clear that he had already given up, but she had no intention of doing so.

"I'm not going to have you hanging around the jail in the hope of seeing him," Bob said testily, as the car containing Cal and two of the state policemen drove off down the road. The other state car followed it, lights pulsing.

"Look, he's entitled to a lawyer, isn't he? I'll bring one to the jail. You have to let him have a legal conference, that's his right," Lara said.

Bob's eyes narrowed. "What lawyer?" he said.

"Norman Oakland, Rose's lawyer."

"Norman Oakland is an estate lawyer!" Bob said incredulously. "What the hell is he going to do?"

"He can take notes and get the ball rolling for whoever takes over for him later. If he's passed the bar he knows more than I do. I'll have him there before five."

Bob stared at her pityingly. "You're making a fool of yourself, Lara."

"That's my concern, isn't it? And you should know, Bob, that I'll be watching your treatment of Cal very carefully, and I won't hesitate to file a complaint if your personal feelings about this case result in any unfairness.''

''My personal feelings about this case?'' Bob inquired carefully, his eyes locked with hers.

''Oh, come on, Bob. I'm sure you decided to investigate Cal in the first place because I preferred him to you. If we had marched off into the sunset together you wouldn't have cared if Cal was Bluebeard or the Boston Strangler. You never would have checked his record.''

''I investigated your boyfriend because he was a suspicious character,'' Bob said tightly.

''Oh, really? He was here for two months before I showed up and you didn't seem to find anything suspicious about him during that time. He was minding his own business and working hard. As I recall, you were friendly toward him the day Jerry Perkins accosted me. In fact, you didn't suspect Cal's true criminal nature until Rose's funeral made it clear that he was your rival for my affections.''

Bob turned beet red, but he was still determined to keep up the facade of an officer of the law doing his duty. ''You flatter yourself a great deal,'' he said grimly, ''and I'm sorry you insist on injecting personal feelings into this. It's not my fault that your boyfriend turned out to be a wanted fugitive, and giving me a hard time isn't going to make him innocent.''

And it wasn't going to help Cal to infuriate Bob, Lara realized, sorry that she had shot off her mouth without thinking. As always when upset, she had talked too much.

"You're right, Bob. Only a review of his case can do that, and you can be sure I'll be working on it. I'll see you at the jail." She went back inside and picked up the phone to dial Norman Oakland's number. As she listened to his secretary tell her that the lawyer was in court, she heard Bob's police car pull away from the front of the house.

"Please tell Mr. Oakland to meet me as soon as possible at the county jail," Lara told the secretary. "I'll need him to talk to my friend, who's been arrested, and to give me an immediate referral to a criminal attorney."

When she finished the call Lara grabbed her purse and keys from the front hall table and dashed for the door. She was operating on automatic pilot, going from one task to the next, not allowing herself to really consider what had just happened or she knew she would start screaming.

Bob was standing just inside the door of the jail when she arrived. He looked at her and said, "Where's the lawyer?"

"He'll be here. Can I see Cal?"

Bob didn't answer.

"Well?" Lara said.

"I told you that he could see his lawyer, not you," Bob replied flatly.

"Come on, Bob. If this is within your jurisdiction, give me a break. You've got him locked up. He's not going anywhere. Can't you give me a few minutes with him in the visitor's room?"

Two other cops were standing nearby, listening, and it may have been their presence that finally forced Bob to say, "All right. Ten minutes, that's it. Alice searches you and then the guard stands outside the door the whole time."

"Fine," Lara said.

He led her to a small anteroom, where a policewoman patted her down and then confiscated her purse. After that Bob took her through a narrow hall floored with gray tile and painted an institutional green. At the end of it was a small room that contained a scarred wooden table and scattered plastic chairs. The door featured a frosted glass panel and a brass peephole, and as it closed behind her she could see a uniformed policeman take up his position next to it.

"Ten," Bob said again, flashing his fingers at her. He left the room by another door, and shortly after he disappeared through it, Cal came in, still handcuffed, escorted by another guard.

"Sit there, Churchill," the cop said. "I can see you through that window," he added, pointing. "If you move from that seat I'll be on you in a flash." He pulled the second door closed behind him.

"Cal, Norman Oakland will be here shortly," Lara said, covering his hand with her own. "Everything is going to be all right."

He pulled his fingers away from hers.

"Cal, don't shut me out. We can fight this together, and we'll win. I know you didn't do anything wrong. You couldn't deliberately hurt anyone. I can take a loan against the ranch—there's still some equity in it—and get the best lawyer..." Lara knew she was babbling, anything to avoid the awful look of finality on his face, but she couldn't stop talking until he held up his hand.

"Lara, it's over," he said quietly. "It was the best while it lasted, but I'm not going to drag you into my disaster. I never lied to you, I always told you that. I came in here just to see you one last time and say goodbye."

Lara stared at him. "Goodbye?" she whispered.

"Yes. You have to let this go, to let *me* go. I'm not going to have you run up debts on my account, chase me back east, hang on to an illusion of hope that will only make you hate me in the end when reality comes crashing in on you. I'm an accused murderer. Soon I'll be a convicted felon. It's finished, you must see that."

"Don't you love me anymore?"

For the first time his steely gaze faltered. "That doesn't matter," he said, looking away from her.

"It's the only thing that *does* matter!" Lara cried.

Cal closed his eyes. "I almost refused to see you, because I knew you would be like this, I knew you wouldn't..." He stopped, clenching his manacled hands.

"Wouldn't what?" she prompted.

"Give up on me," he said quietly.

"Of course I won't give up on you! What kind of person would I be if I ran out on you when the chips were down?"

"The chips aren't down, Lara, they're gone. I'm busted flat, at the end of my rope, there's no place else to go. Instead of facing the charges against me in a case I couldn't win, I did a stupid thing. I ran away. Our justice system doesn't look kindly on people who do that, and I'm not going to let you ruin your life and throw away your inheritance trying to straighten out my mess."

"But, Cal, maybe it *is* possible to help you. Can't you tell me about your case, give me some idea how I can help?"

"No," he said, his mouth a grim line.

Faced with his implacability, Lara tried another tactic. "Then what am I supposed to do with the rest of my life?" she asked.

"Find somebody else," he said.

"I see. Somebody like Bob Trask out there, some solid citizen like him? You once told me you couldn't stand the thought of him touching me. Can you stand it now? Can you picture another man making me gasp, and shudder, and cry out with pleasure? Can you?"

"Stop it," he said hoarsely, grinding his teeth.

"Tell me something. You knew Bob was jealous. Didn't you wonder if he might try to find out about you?"

"I thought it was a strong possibility, especially after you told me what had happened between the two of you," he said dully.

"And yet you stayed," she said.

"I couldn't leave you," he said simply. "Having just a few more days with you was worth the risk of getting caught."

"You can say that to me and then expect me to abandon you?" she said, starting to cry. "Why didn't you tell me the truth? I would have run away with you...we could have gone anywhere together."

He shook his head. "That kind of life would be no good for you, running, hiding, always looking over your shoulder. Believe me, I know. I couldn't turn you into a fugitive."

"This is better?" she demanded in amazement, almost laughing through her tears. What kind of logic was dictating his actions?

"Yes, it is," he replied firmly. "You're innocent of any crime. You weren't harboring a fugitive because you didn't know I was one. All you knew was that I had a problem in my past, and that can be said of a lot of people. As long as I didn't tell you anything specific, you were protected. I knew you wouldn't try to ferret out the details on your own because you really didn't want to know any more than I wanted to tell you."

"But don't you see that I have to know now?" Lara said. "I have to know in order to help you."

"You're not going to help me. You're free and clear. You can walk away from all of this now, go on with your life and let me deal with my situation alone."

"I'm not walking away..." Lara began, and then fell silent as the cop guarding the outer door pulled it open suddenly and stuck his head into the room.

"Time's up," he said.

Cal rose immediately and said to the second guard, who had opened the door leading back to the cells, "I'm ready."

"Cal, wait..." Lara began.

The first guard put his hand on her arm, restraining her. Lara was forced to watch as Cal left the room without a backward glance.

The guard's hand fell away. "Let's go, miss," he said.

She followed him back to the reception area, where the policewoman handed Lara her purse and Norman Oakland was waiting with Bob Trask.

"Oh, Mr. Oakland, I'm so glad to see you," Lara said, grasping at any straw. "Did you tell Bob you were here to see my friend?"

The lawyer glanced at Bob, who said, "He's refused to see Norman, Lara."

Lara looked at Oakland, who nodded. "I'm sorry, Lara, but if a client declines my services there's nothing I can do."

"Maybe another attorney..." Lara murmured desperately.

"He says he doesn't want one," Bob interjected. "I think you should go home, Lara."

Lara sat on a bench in the hall and wondered where that was. Rose was gone from the ranch and now Cal was gone, too.

Where was home?

Lara tried to get in to see Cal again for the next three days, but he consistently refused to see her. Norman Oakland had no better luck, and on the fourth day Cal was flown to Hartford in the company of a deputy sheriff to face the charges against him there.

When Lara learned that Cal had been transferred

to Connecticut, she knew that she would have to take some drastic action to make sure he didn't slip through her fingers forever. She met with her real estate agent and withdrew the ranch from the market, and then, with Norman Oakland's help, got a loan against the property to finance her future activities. She closed up the house and, leaving the business in Jim Stampley's capable hands, flew to the school district outside Chicago where she had been employed for the past five years. There she had the unenviable task of persuading the Board of Education to grant her a leave of absence when the start of the academic year was only a few days away. Luckily Lara had tenure as well as a spotless record, and the student teacher she had supervised the previous semester was only too happy to take over for her. By the time Lara had settled her job, and returned to her apartment to pack for the trip to Hartford, she felt that she had established some small measure of control over the situation.

Cal might still refuse to see her, but she could hire the lawyer whose name she had obtained from Norman Oakland's son to look into Cal's case. She still didn't know what had happened to him, and until she understood the details she was working in the dark.

Hartford looked like every other Northeastern city Lara had seen, with a hectic, traffic-choked business and shopping district, its clogged side streets still in the grip of late summer heat in early September. Lara entered a gray stone office building and consulted the roster of professional listings posted on the wall next to the elevator. Carol Novak, the classmate of Norman Oakland's son, had an office on the third floor. As Lara rode up to see the lawyer she wondered, for the hundredth time, what she would learn from the visit.

Carol Novak was a slim brunette in her mid-thirties who rose from her desk to shake Lara's hand firmly as she entered the lawyer's office.

"Please have a seat," Carol said. "I have quite a story to tell you."

Lara sat with her purse in her lap, her fingers twisting the buckle on it nervously.

"When Walter Oakland called me, and then I received your letter, I debated whether or not I should get involved in this," Novak began, opening up a file on her desk. "A client who doesn't want a lawyer isn't a client, but in actual fact I am representing you, not Churchill, so I requested your friend's records from the Hartford Superior Court. I understood from our correspondence that you know very little about this man's background or his troubles with the law?"

Lara nodded, feeling ridiculous.

Novak raised one manicured eyebrow. "I must say you have a great deal of faith in this person, to have come so far and spent so much time on him when you're operating in a near vacuum."

"I feel very strongly that he couldn't have intentionally harmed anyone. I may not know all the details of his past, but I know him."

Novak nodded. "Well, your confidence may be justified. From what I've read, your friend's tale is a pretty dismal one, and the last incident that put him on the wrong side of the law was just the latest episode in a long history of unkind fate and bad luck."

Lara said nothing, listening intently.

"I'm going to give you a copy of this file, so you can read it all for yourself, but it may help to move this along if I summarize. Is that all right with you?"

Lara nodded.

"Caleb Churchill was abandoned as an infant at a convent in West Hartford, where he was raised in a parish orphanage. He was fostered out, then returned, and as an adolescent he was transferred to a farm in Winstead dedicated to the care of similarly situated children. He left that facility at the age of seventeen, when he petitioned to be declared an emancipated minor and the state could no longer hold him. He entered the construction industry as a day laborer and worked in and around Hartford for twelve years without incident, working his way up to become a site supervisor at the time of the altercation that resulted in his current difficulties."

"And what was that?" Lara asked, thinking again about all the lonely years Cal spent in the care of strangers. No wonder Rose's concern had meant so much to him.

"Apparently, as a means of earning some extra money, he took up Golden Gloves boxing and became quite good, winning several local titles," Novak continued. "The importance of this seemingly innocuous tidbit will become obvious later. Anyway, one night a couple of years ago while Churchill was having a drink after work in The Foundry, which is a bar about five blocks from here, he noticed a wild kid making a pest of himself with one of the barmaids Churchill knew. He intervened to help her and the situation escalated, with the drunken kid refusing to back down and goading your friend into a fight. Blows were exchanged, and after one of them, the drunk fell and hit his head on one of the metal guardrails around the bar, fracturing his skull. He died instantly. At the hospital Churchill discovered that his antagonist was Congressman Winterfield's son, out on the town with his Trinity prep school buddies."

Novak looked up from her notes, but Lara couldn't comment; her mind was spinning, trying to process the new information.

"It will help you to know that the Winterfield family is something of an institution around here, old money, over on the Mayflower, public service, Yale, that sort of thing," Novak said dryly. "You can imagine what someone like Churchill, raised in this area and with his disadvantaged background, thought when he realized who he was up against."

"He thought his goose was cooked," Lara said softly.

"Exactly. And he was right. The best he could have hoped for was a ruling of death by misadventure from the coroner's inquiry, but he quickly found himself charged with second-degree murder rather than the more common charge of manslaughter usual in such an incident. Winterfield's high-priced lawyer argued that Cal's hands were lethal weapons as a result of his boxing training. With little or no resources of his own and with Winterfield working full-time to put him away for the death of his only son, Churchill felt that his way out of the tangle was to run."

Lara sighed. "The cop who arrested him in Montana told me that he knocked out a guard when he was being transferred from one jail to another." Novak nodded. "That's an assault charge in and of itself, isn't it?" Lara said dismally.

"Desperate times, desperate measures," Novak said, shrugging. "I would argue in this case that murder charges should never have been filed. There were enough witnesses who said that the death was clearly accidental, and that the aggressor was unquestionably the Winterfield boy, who antagonized your friend physically to the point that striking back at him was self-defense."

"Do you mean there's hope?" Lara asked eagerly, hardly daring to believe it.

Novak held up her hand. "I can't promise you anything. I'm merely saying that a good case could be made that your friend's treatment was prejudicial. His hearing judge was a golf partner of the Congressman's brother, who practices law in Avon, and the depositions of many of the witnesses were dismissed at the arraignment as irrelevant, when in my opinion they definitely went to the question of intent, which is crucial in a murder case."

"Could you get the case reopened, try to get the original charge dismissed?" Lara asked breathlessly.

"I don't know. The first thing we would need is your friend's cooperation, which at this point we don't have."

"I'll get it," Lara said firmly.

"He's a proven fugitive so they probably won't let him post bond. You'll have to get in to see him at the jail."

"I'll do it."

"All right. I'll say this much, I think you have a chance. Congressman Winterfield is now dead, and the hearing judge has retired and moved to Arizona. Those two factors could help you immensely, since the only surviving member of the immediate Winterfield family is the dead boy's sister, and she lives in Italy. It is unlikely she would even hear about a review of the case, and if she did, I doubt she would come back here for it since she and the brother never got along. They were half siblings, same father, different mothers. And since the hearing judge is now off the bench anyone else reviewing the case would be more likely to point out errors. There's no chance of offending a sitting judge who might retaliate or whose career might suffer. Get the picture?"

"I've got it," Lara said.

Novak sat back in her chair and surveyed Lara speculatively. "You do realize that I will have to charge you for the time spent on this case even if Churchill refuses to let me represent him?"

"Yes."

"You must love him very much. I gather his detachment from this effort is his way of expressing his affection for you? Self-sacrifice and all that?"

"Yes," Lara said again.

Novak sighed and closed the file. "Well, you have all the facts now. Do what you can. I know a younger, liberal judge who resents the stranglehold

Winterfield and his clique had on justice in these local courts for too long. He'd be a good one to approach. I know his clerk, too, which is even better—I can get the brief read fast. But you have to talk to Churchill and bring him in on it, yesterday. The Lord helps those who help themselves."

"I didn't realize you were divine," Lara said, smiling for the first time during the interview.

"Almost," Novak said, smiling back. She stood to indicate that the meeting was over.

Lara rose also and said, "I'll be in touch."

Novak nodded. "Make it fast. They'll process him real quick. He was a fugitive for a year and that makes them look bad. They'll want him under lock and key. I have to get in there waving my paperwork before he's shipped up the river, so to speak. Understand?"

"I understand."

"Good luck."

Lara walked out of the lawyer's office feeling, if not hopeful, at least as if a burden had been lifted.

There was a chance, and she was going to make sure Caleb Churchill took it.

Getting in to see Cal proved to be more difficult than she had anticipated. The jail in Hartford had a preset visitors' list, and Cal had not cleared anyone to visit him. Carol Novak had to intervene and get special permission to contact him on a pro bono basis, and Cal was apparently so shocked that Novak was already filing a brief in his case that he agreed to meet with her. She explained Lara's role in procuring her services and then, five weeks after he was transferred to Hartford, Lara was finally granted permission to visit.

The cool breath of autumn was blowing though the Connecticut valley as she parked her rental car at a meter and fed it as many coins as it would take. The jail was downtown, and the weak Indian Summer sun warmed her back as she walked two city blocks and then entered the jail.

It was a Sunday afternoon and the waiting room was packed. Lara was amazed at the number of young families with children waiting to see prisoners, but she was too edgy to dwell on the tragedy and sadness that fact implied. Her hands were like ice and she hadn't eaten for two days. She knew that she had done everything possible to get Cal to change his mind; if he was seeing her this time just to dismiss her once more it was really and truly over.

It seemed as if she sat in the noisy room for a very long time, and when she was finally admitted with a group of about ten other people, she hung back, nervous now that the moment she had been working for had finally come. Their identification was checked again as they passed through an electronic gate, and then they were led to an open room with many tables, where six armed guards stood at various points, arms folded, eyes wary.

The children rushed forward to see their loved ones, and Lara looked around for Cal. She finally spotted him, seated alone at the table farthest from the door. He stood as she approached him, and she could see at a glance that more than his tan had faded. He looked taut, drained, devoid of spirit and destitute of hope.

Well, she was going to change all that. If he would let her.

"Hi, Cal," she said softly, wanting to kiss him but holding herself back.

He shook his head slightly. "Lara, what are you doing here?" he replied.

"You know what I'm doing here," she said brightly. "Carol Novak told you."

"Carol Novak is a lawyer. She's just taking your money. She gets paid by the hour. She'll run up a tab chasing a wild goose to the depths of Siberia if you'll foot the bill for it."

Lara tried to keep up her courage, but she was daunted. This wasn't the way she had hoped it would go.

"Novak is ethical, Cal. Norman Oakland's son went to law school with her. She was very frank with me during our first meeting and told me exactly what we were up against. But she also said some things had changed since you were charged, and that the deposition of several mitigating witnesses had been ignored by the judge at your preliminary hearing."

Cal closed his eyes. "I know all that, Lara, better than you do. I'm still in jail."

"But don't you want to try? I've gone to all this trouble to get a lawyer interested in your case, and you're just going to blow it off? Don't I mean enough to you to try?"

He opened his eyes but didn't look at her. "I just can't go through it all again, and lose again, this time with you at ringside. It was humiliating enough the first time, with you watching the whole thing it would be unbearable."

Lara stared at him. "I see. Your pride is going to prevent us from having a future together. That makes a lot of sense."

He didn't answer.

Lara decided to change her course of action. Trying to reason with him while he was in this frame of mind was fruitless, so she opted for another tactic.

"All right, Cal. I can see that you've made your decision, and after over a month of running around trying to get you a new hearing, I'm a little tired. I'm really not in the mood for your self-pity, so if it's all the same to you I'm just going to leave." She turned back toward the door, clutching her purse, her fingers white.

Her heart was pounding and her mouth was dry. She knew that she was taking a terrible chance; he might just let her walk right out the door, and out of his life.

She heard his quick step behind her, and when she turned he drew her into his arms.

"Don't go," he said softly. "I'm sorry, don't go." He kissed her cheek, then her mouth, and Lara melted against him.

The guard who had stepped forward when Cal grabbed Lara's arm relaxed and moved back when he saw that Lara was not resisting. When Cal released Lara he took her hand and led her back to the table, where she sat and he took a chair next to her.

"Listen," he said, taking in Lara's wet eyes and trembling chin. "I want to be with you more than I've ever wanted anything in my life. It's just hard for me to believe that it's even possible. Can you understand that?''

"I understand,'' Lara replied softly, taking his hand. "Carol Novak filled me in on your background and I can appreciate that you don't expect to get a break, since you've never had any. But meeting me was a break, wasn't it? Maybe it's the beginning of a new trend. Maybe things will be different from now on. I know I sound like Pollyanna, but you have to have faith or there's no chance for us. I can't do it all alone.''

"You won't have to do it alone, Lara,'' he said. "If you can come from Montana to Connecticut, postpone your job and convince a lawyer to take on my sorry case, the least I can do is work with you.''

"Thank you,'' Lara said primly.

"I need to make love to you so badly,'' he said quietly, twining his fingers with hers. "I want to throw everybody out of this room and do it right here.''

"I'm afraid that's not going to get you any closer to freedom,'' Lara said firmly, alarmed by the dangerous light that had come into his eyes.

"Nothing is,'' he said glumly. "Even I know I'm a bad candidate for bail.''

Lara leaned forward eagerly. "Maybe not. Carol thought so at first, too, but when she filed for a new hearing the court clerk told her that particular judge has previously granted bail to some people whose flight was the result of an unfair arrest, so—''

"Lara, I bolted,'' he said flatly, interrupting her. "They're not going to forget that.''

"All the same, we're going to try, right?" Lara said, inclining her head to make the point.

He nodded wearily.

"So let's proceed on the assumption that you will get out on bail and join me at the residence inn where we will, number one, make up for lost time, and number two, plan the strategy for obtaining your release," Lara said lightly.

"What the hell is a residence inn?" Cal asked.

"It's a sort of hotel for transferred executives who need a place to stay before they move permanently," Lara replied. "Carol found it for me. It's cheaper than staying in a hotel and the room has a hot plate and fridge. Kind of like your loft back at El Cielo."

"You've disrupted your whole life for me," he said softly.

"I don't mind. I have no life without you. The only thing that bothers me is your giving up before we start."

"No more of that, I promise."

"Good. Now let's talk about exactly what happened the night the Winterfield boy died. Carol said that it's important for you to remember every detail, any little thing might help us."

"Like I could forget," he said darkly.

Lara whipped a notebook out of her purse, then glanced at the clock displayed prominently in the common room. "We have twenty minutes. Let's go."

Cal began to talk and she began to write.

Ten days after her visit to the jail Lara learned that Carol Novak had obtained a bail hearing for Cal.

Seven

Cal stared up at the cracked plaster ceiling of his cell and wondered if there really was a chance that he might get out of this place, for good. He loved Lara desperately, but she was an optimist. Her well-tended childhood spent in the care of a loving family had given her a rosy outlook that he did not share. He was always surprised when he walked down the street and lightning did not strike him. This time it had, again, in the person of Bob Trask, but if it hadn't been Trask it would have been someone or something else. He had landed back where society said he belonged—in jail.

And unlike Lara, he didn't think his chances of getting out were very good. But then again, he hadn't believed that she'd come to Connecticut and hire a lawyer and get him a bail review, and all of that had happened. So maybe there was some hope that the judge at the hearing today would let him go.

Cal sat up on his bunk and looked around the tiny room, which held, in addition to his bed, a sink, a toilet, and the covered tin plate that had contained his breakfast. As he watched a hand snaked through the little door in the bars of his cell and grabbed the metal dish. He heard the rattling of metal as a kitchen worker wheeled a cart down the hall outside his cell, collecting plates. In a few minutes he would be herded along with the others down to the shower room, and then, since he was due in court at nine, he would be permitted to skip exercise in the yard and go directly to the common room. There he would meet the two guards who would take him to court.

He hadn't seen Lara since her last visit, and he was looking forward, as always, to her fresh beauty and calming presence, but he couldn't bear to think of her searing disappointment if his bail was denied. She seemed to think that if she just worked hard enough, everything would turn out the way she wanted; her attitude reflected the faith of a five-year-old, and it was endearing, but hardly realistic. She didn't have any experience with the pitiless monolith of the justice system, or how it treated people like himself.

He was afraid she was in for a rude awakening, but then, she had already survived one of those, and she still loved him.

Maybe another miracle was on the way.

Lara entered the courtroom with Carol Novak and looked past the empty rows of benches to the front, where the stenographer was sitting down at her machine and the bailiff was dusting the judge's bench. The butterflies in her stomach were zooming in full flight and she was fighting back waves of nausea. She looked on, taking her seat, as Cal was led into the courtroom by two guards, one of whom unlocked his handcuffs and pulled out a chair for him at the defendant's table. He sat, looking around for Lara. She waved to him from the first row, trying to display a bravery she couldn't quite manufacture at the moment. The only other occupant of the courtroom was the state's attorney named Canfield, who was a short young man with a slight build, pale skin and ginger hair. He didn't look old enough to vote, much less represent the District Attorney's Office, but he had a brisk, efficient manner that belied his youthful appearance. Lara was sure he knew what he was doing.

The bailiff told them all to rise as the judge entered from a side door; then the bailiff announced the name and number of the case. Lara saw Cal swallow hard and look down at his hands.

He was wearing the same clothes he had purchased from Maisie Trask in Murphysburg, which Lara had brought from Montana. The jacket hung a little loosely on him, but Lara saw the recorder, a pretty young woman with chestnut hair, glance at him with poorly veiled interest as he rose to face the judge.

Even when under arrest, Cal managed to convey a powerful magnetism.

The judge, whose name was Mellon, riffled

through a stack of papers on his desk and then said, "We are here to consider the question of bail for one Caleb Churchill in the previously named action." He looked up and peered over his Ben Franklin glasses at Carol Novak.

"Miss Novak, we will hear from you first," he said.

Carol rose and stepped up to the podium, placing a stack of note cards on it and clearing her throat.

"Your Honor, as you stated, we are here to consider the matter of bail in the case of Caleb Churchill, who is charged with second-degree murder in the death of Matthew Winterfield. It is our contention that Mr. Churchill should never have been charged in this action, since there is ample evidence that the death was accidental. The depositions of exculpatory witnesses were not even considered at Mr. Churchill's arraignment. The lesser charge of involuntary manslaughter was dismissed in favor of the more serious murder charge, even though the activity which resulted in the death of Mr. Winterfield was completely without Mr. Churchill's willful intent. We therefore request that the defendant be granted a reasonable bail in the amount of twenty-five thousand dollars, pending his new hearing on the dismissal of the murder charge."

Judge Mellon looked at Canfield. "Mr. Canfield? What do the People have to say about that?"

"Your Honor, the very existence of this hearing is an outrage," Canfield began. "Miss Novak neglected to mention that Mr. Churchill has been at large for over a year, a fugitive from justice in this matter. He assaulted a guard at the Enfield Correctional Facility in order to effect his escape, which is further evidence of his violent nature, and was only returned to this jurisdiction when an alert police officer in Montana checked into his background and realized Churchill was wanted in Connecticut. It would be ludicrous for Miss Novak to argue that Churchill is not a flight risk, since he ran once before, and to save the state the expense of tracking him down again I request that the defendant be denied bail.''

The judge sighed and removed his glasses. He ran his hand over his grizzled gray hair and then gazed at Carol, his expression one of strained tolerance.

''Miss Novak?''

''Your Honor, please consider that the charges against this defendant were wrongfully lodged and may be completely dismissed at his upcoming hearing,'' Carol began.

''I wouldn't jump to that conclusion, Miss Novak,'' Judge Mellon said dryly.

''You yourself have ruled that his case warrants a review,'' Carol said pointedly to him.

''Don't remind me of my previous rulings, Miss Novak. I'm not senile yet and being treated as if I have that infirmity makes me liable to change my mind,'' the judge said sharply.

The knot in Lara's gut tightened another notch.

''I'm sorry, Your Honor,'' Carol said quietly. ''But you must concede that the defendant should not have been charged in the first place and the gravity of his situation led to the panic which resulted in his flight. He felt that he could not possibly get a fair hearing and his only choice was to run."

"Most defendants feel that way, Miss Novak, but most don't knock guards unconscious and flee the state."

Canfield smiled slightly; Lara wanted to punch him.

"Begging your pardon, Your Honor, but most defendants are not in the position Mr. Churchill occupied at that time," Carol said calmly. "The victim in this case was Matthew Winterfield, and his father, the late Congressman Winterfield, brought all of his resources to bear to make sure that the defendant was charged with the maximum—"

"Your Honor, I object," Canfield interrupted her. "The identity of the victim in this case is irrelevant. This is a bail hearing and the sole issue for consideration should be whether or not the defendant is a flight risk, which he has already proven to be. Therefore—"

Judge Mellon held up his hand, the pale skin of his palm contrasting with the rich brown of his fingers.

"Mr. Canfield, I will decide which issues to consider in this hearing," the judge said. "I will hear from the People when Miss Novak has finished. Until that time, let her talk."

Canfield subsided, shuffling through his yellow legal pad, looking mildly annoyed.

"Thank you, Your Honor," Carol said. "It is of course my contention that the identity of the victim was and is relevant, especially with respect to the state of mind of Mr. Churchill at the time he fled the state. You know his background—I included a summary of it in the brief I submitted to your clerk."

Judge Mellon grunted.

"Obviously, someone raised under the circumstances Mr. Churchill experienced, who spent his whole life up to that time in this area where the Winterfields were so prominent, would feel he had no chance to beat the charges, no matter how inappropriate they were."

Canfield squeaked, but the judge silenced him with one severe look.

Cal was staring at the wall next to the judge's head; he obviously didn't like this discussion of his previous "circumstances." Lara knew that the very thought of someone pitying him would make him see red, but it was part of Carol's strategy to make the judge understand the motivation for Cal's actions.

"From Mr. Churchill's point of view, all he had done was intervene to stop a snotty kid who was annoying a friend of his, and the next thing he knew he was charged with murder, the murder of the only son of one of the state's wealthiest men," Carol continued. "He had no way to combat Martin Winterfield's nearly infinite resources, and when he saw that the hearing judge was a Winterfield friend, and that the depositions his lawyer had gathered were disregarded, he saw his prospects as hopeless. Can you blame him?"

Canfield made a disgusted sound. Judge Mellon looked at him. "What do the People have to say to that, Mr. Canfield?"

"Your Honor, Miss Novak is skilfully shifting the subject of this hearing away from Mr. Churchill's escape to a discussion of his underprivileged childhood. If every defendant who had a miserable upbringing was permitted to use that as an excuse for unlawful flight we wouldn't be able to deny bail to anyone! It's ridiculous, and a complete perversion of this process. The People reiterate their request for denial of bail in this matter."

Judge Mellon sat back in his chair, surveying the players before him. He looked at Cal. "I think I would like to hear from the defendant," he said.

Lara glanced at Carol, who turned and gestured for Cal to rise from his seat. He stood, staring back at the judge warily.

"Mr. Churchill, what do you have to say for yourself?" the judge asked.

Cal looked at Lara, then back at the judge. "I didn't kill anyone, Your Honor. It happened just like Miss Novak says. The Winterfield kid was making a nuisance of himself and I tried to stop him. He was drunk, he kept swinging at me, he finally connected and I got mad, I guess, and popped him one back. I didn't hit him hard, but he was already rocky from the booze and he just dropped like a stone. I didn't realize he had hit his head until I bent to pick him up and saw..." He stopped.

"What?" the judge asked.

"Blood," Cal said softly.

"Your Honor, may I remind you once more that this is a *bail* hearing," Canfield interjected in a tone of exaggerated patience. "These are substantive issues and should be reserved for the hearing on the charges which is set for October 20. I protest—"

"Oh, be quiet, Canfield," the judge snapped. "The state has awarded me great latitude in these proceedings, and if I want to hear this testimony now, I will. You can file an objection with the judicial review board if you like."

Canfield rolled his eyes, but shut up, not wanting to risk a contempt citation.

"So you maintain that your attack on Matthew Winterfield was provoked," the judge said to Cal.

"Yes, sir, it was. And I had plenty of people who saw it and were willing to say so, but nobody would listen to them."

"And that's why you ran?"

Cal nodded.

"I am not an advocate of flight to avoid prosecution," Judge Mellon said slowly, "but in this situation—"

"What about the assault on the prison guard?" Canfield yelped incredulously, amazed that the judge was even listening to this.

"'But for causation,' Your Honor," Carol said quickly. "But for the wrongful arrest, Mr. Churchill never would have been in custody, never would have been forced to flee—"

"Forced to flee?" Canfield screeched, his voice rising comically. "Nobody forced this man to do anything! Your Honor, this is a scandal, and I must register the outrage of the People that an arrestee with an established record of violence and a history of flight should even be given this consideration—"

"I've got the picture, Mr. Canfield. You know which forms to file to state your displeasure for the record. But for the moment, I'm going to take a chance."

Lara sat forward, her pulse racing.

"Bail is granted to the defendant in the amount of twenty-five thousand dollars, cash or bond." Mellon banged his gavel.

Canfield threw up his hands in disgust, knocking his legal pad to the floor.

Lara shot out of her seat and embraced Carol, who patted her on the back. Lara then wanted to go to Cal, but she wasn't sure if courtroom protocol would permit it.

"Not so fast, Miss Novak," the judge said warningly to Carol, who was clearly elated.

The attorney released Lara and looked back at the judge, her expression apprehensive.

"If this man disappears," he said, stabbing his finger at Cal, "I will hold you personally responsible. There will be no hole deep enough to hide you from my wrath. Is that clear?"

"Yes, your honor," Carol said meekly.

"You are getting a break here, son, maybe one of the few you've ever gotten," the judge said sternly, now addressing Cal. "Don't blow it."

"I won't, Your Honor."

Judge Mellon nodded. "With Miss Novak's help, bail should be arranged in a couple of hours, at which time you will be released. Bailiff, you may remove the prisoner."

Lara shot Cal a triumphant glance as he was escorted out of the courtroom, and he grinned back at her, dazed but happy.

"Novak, you're a magician," Canfield said, as he snapped the locks on his briefcase. "I never would have believed that this fiasco of a result was possible."

"Believe it."

"Only Judge Mellon would have listened to your sob story," Canfield added snidely. "He thinks every doper on the street deserves a second chance."

"Some of them do," Carol replied crisply, and steered Lara past the losing attorney.

"What's his problem?" Lara asked, once they were in the hall. "He's behaving like you knifed his mother."

"Almost. Canfield may look twelve and act like William Shatner, but until today he's never lost at a bail hearing."

"I'm glad you didn't tell me that before we went in there," Lara said, shuddering.

"I didn't think you'd need that extra pressure," Carol said dryly. "Now, I know a bondsman who works fast and who will take my word for the trustworthiness of my client." She smiled. "Have you got twenty-five thousand dollars?"

"You bet."

"Then let's go spring your boyfriend."

Lara was waiting when Cal was released that afternoon. She watched as the guard uncuffed him and handed him a large manila envelope. Cal stuck it under his arm, then waited for the buzzer that signaled the release of the gate. It sounded shrilly, and the door swung open automatically.

He stepped through it and into Lara's arms.

"I don't deserve you," he said huskily, pressing her close.

"Yes, you do," she replied, reveling in the well remembered strength of his arms. She missed him every moment she wasn't with him.

"Let's get the hell out of here," he said, glancing over his shoulder at their audience. "Where's your car?"

"About ten miles away," Lara replied ruefully. "I had to park in Guatemala." She pointed in the direction of the lot.

"That's more than ten miles away," he said, as they passed thorough the door and onto the street. He stopped and took a deep breath of the early autumn air.

"Freedom," he said. "It smells great."

"It smells like downtown Hartford, exhaust fumes and coal tar and cement dust."

"Not to me," he said, and picked her up, spinning her in a wide circle.

"Caleb, put me down this instant," Lara said, as one of her shoes fell off.

He retrieved the pump and she slipped her foot into it.

"What does this remind you of?" she said, laughing. "Prince Charming and Cinderella!"

"The Frog Prince, you mean," he replied, straightening. As he did so he dropped his envelope.

"What's in there?" Lara asked.

"Personal effects. Watch, wallet, coins, etc. When you finally get out they thoughtfully return whatever they confiscated."

"So, what shall we do now?" Lara asked mischievously, casting a sidelong glance at him.

"I think you can guess what I want to do," he said, enfolding her and kissing her neck.

"My temporary abode is only ten minutes away," she informed him.

"Let's run to the car," he suggested, grabbing her hand.

They did, and were at Lara's apartment within half an hour. Cal didn't even look at the layout, except to locate the bedroom and lead Lara to the bed. He undressed her and himself simultaneously, pulling off his tie and unzipping her dress in almost the same motion, flinging clothes onto the floor and furniture with indecent abandon. When Lara was down to her underwear he set her on the edge of the bed and peeled off her lingerie, kissing her breasts when he removed her bra, pushing her backward with the palm of his hand when he had removed her briefs. She lay naked, ready to receive him, reaching for him eagerly when he was still wearing his pants and pulling him on top of her.

"Can't wait, huh?" he murmured, as she fumbled with the buckle of his belt.

"No," she admitted, sighing as he pressed her down into the mattress and she felt his arousal. She played with the clasp a little more, then said in frustration, "I give up. Is there a magic word?"

He chuckled softly, then stood up and discarded

his trousers. When he lay down again he embraced her and said into her ear, "Ready?"

"Oh, yes."

He drove into her so deeply that she moaned aloud with gratification.

"Did you miss me?" he said huskily, as she wrapped her legs around him tightly.

"More than you can imagine."

"I don't have to imagine," he said softly. "I know."

They were both too hungry to go slowly, and when it was over Lara lay against his shoulder, listening to his heartbeat return to normal. She thought he was asleep when he said suddenly, "This is a pretty nice place."

"Thinking of taking a lease?" Lara said teasingly.

"No, I mean it. I'm glad you haven't been living in a dump while all this was going on."

"I didn't think you noticed anything except the whereabouts of the sack."

"I'm noticing it right now. There's a living room through that door..."

"Very good."

"And a bathroom that way..." He pointed.

"Yes."

"And I know I passed a little kitchen on the way in here."

"You get a gold star."

"Speaking of kitchens..." he began.

Lara turned her head to look up at him inquiringly.

"Is there any food in yours?" he asked.

"Not unless you consider half a lemon, a jar of mustard and a bottle of mineral water food."

Cal groaned.

"There are several take-out places nearby," Lara said.

He brightened. "Really?"

"Really. What do you think I've been living on? I haven't exactly been cooking gourmet meals."

"Do they deliver?"

"Some do."

He sat up and grabbed the phone. "Pizza, burgers, Chinese?" he asked.

"The Crimson Pagoda is just a few blocks away. The menu is in the top drawer of the telephone table."

He retrieved the order sheet and dialed the number. "Lo mein okay for you?" he asked. "I remember you like that."

"Fine." Lara listened to him rattle off a long order and then said to him when he hung up the phone, "I assume you're inviting the West Point Drill Team to join us?"

"I've worked up an appetite," he said, grinning. Then his smile faded. "Do you have any money? I think I got six bucks back in the envelope, but that's never going to be enough."

"I have money."

He grew silent, sat up and pulled on his pants. Lara watched him find a cigarette and light it.

"Cal, what is it?" she asked, aware of his change of mood, putting her hand on his arm.

"I hate this whole situation," he said darkly. "I feel like you're keeping me."

"Don't be silly. We're a team. Once this is over I plan to work you to death on the ranch and get back every single dime I've spent in man-hours."

"That isn't funny," he said, not looking at her.

"Why isn't it funny? Don't you plan on going back to Montana with me?" Lara asked.

"Of course I want that more than anything in the world, Lara, but I can't think past my next hearing. Life is in suspended animation until then."

"Can't we just assume that the charges will be dismissed and we'll join forces to bring El Cielo back to its glory days? You're already good with horses. Jim can teach you what you need to know before he goes. I think Rose's fine hand kept the ranch from selling fast so that we could have it once we've cleared up this mess. You have to remember, she's in heaven, sitting at the right hand of God, so she's much more powerful now."

He smiled slightly. "She was powerful enough on earth." He inhaled deeply, causing the tip of the cigarette to glow.

"She knew, Cal. She knew that we should be together."

He nodded silently.

"I think she wanted us to run the ranch after she was gone."

"What about your teaching job?"

Lara shrugged. "I hung onto it with a leave of absence that doesn't end until January, to see what happened with you, but a teacher who could take over for me is already in place. All that's left for me to do is resign.''

''And what will you do if the charges against me aren't dropped?'' Cal asked

''They will be.''

''Lara, answer the question.''

''I'll move here permanently so I can visit you and wait until you get out.''

His grim expression indicated what he thought of that idea. He exhaled a stream of smoke without comment.

''Do we have to talk about it now?'' Lara said quickly, eager to steer clear of dangerous waters. If he got morose about his prospects again it would spoil the occasion. Just his release on bail was cause enough for celebration in her book.

''I guess not,'' he conceded, lifting one shoulder, unwilling to argue when she was so determined to be happy.

''Good. Did I ever tell you about the early morning I spied you swimming at the pond?'' Lara asked teasingly, in a blatant bid to change the subject.

The tactic worked. He looked at her, a faint smile playing around his lips. ''What?'' he said.

''You heard me. I went riding before the sun came up one day and saw you taking a dip before work.''

''I often did that. It was so hot this summer.'' His smile widened. ''How did you react to that scene?''

''I stayed for a while and watched you,'' Lara said.

He laughed. ''A sweet little virgin like yourself? A Peeping Tom?''

''I may have been a virgin, but I was in love.''

"So was I," he said gently, pulling her into his arms.

"A virgin?" Lara asked, but she didn't get the laugh she expected. He drew back to look at her.

"No, not for a long time. When you grow up the way I did you gain lots of experience, but not love. I never had the two together until I met you."

"Then I guess I was lucky," Lara said. "I had the two together from the first."

"Yeah, I'm a real prize package," he said dryly.

"I think so," she said softly, and kissed him.

A very loud knock on the outer door interrupted their conversation.

"Food's here," he said, rising from the bed and stubbing out his cigarette.

"My wallet's in my purse on the chair," Lara called to him as he left the bedroom.

Lara saw his face as he took the money; he wasn't happy. She was beginning to get an appreciation of how difficult this relationship would be for him if he didn't start earning his keep soon.

Cal went into the hall and returned a minute later carrying a brown parcel equipped with two handles.

"I think I've already been locked up too long," he said. "When did they start delivering this stuff in shopping bags?"

"Welcome back to the great Northeast, my love. Is everything in there?"

"Including the Forbidden City, I think." He pulled out box after box and lined them up on the nightstand, finally saying, "You're right. I did get a little carried away."

Lara was laughing, watching him.

"And what's with all these fortune cookies?" he asked, extracting about ten of them from the bag.

"From the size of the order, the packer must have thought you were expecting lots of company."

"Be right back," he said, and disappeared through the bedroom door. When he returned he was carrying plates and silverware, cups and napkins.

"I found everything," he said proudly, dumping his burden on the bed and then handing her a plate.

"That wasn't much of an accomplishment, Cal. The kitchen is the size of a phone booth."

"Don't make fun of a hungry man," he replied, diving into one of the white containers with relish. Silence reigned for quite a while as he ate steadily. When he had consumed his fill he finally observed in a slightly strained voice, "I don't think I can move."

"Don't try. I never knew that you were such a fan of Chinese food."

"I'm a fan of anything that isn't rubber chicken or mystery meat covered with gray sauce. Prison food would put anyone on a permanent diet." He dumped an empty box into the wastebasket and lay back on the bed, his hands behind his head.

"Don't fall asleep," Lara said warningly.

"I wouldn't even consider it," he said, closing his eyes.

"I mean it," Lara said, crawling up next to him on the bed.

He grunted.

"I know how to keep you awake," she murmured, unbuckling his belt and unzipping his fly.

"That'll do it every time," he said, smiling without opening his eyes.

She slipped her hand inside his pants.

He opened his eyes.

"Do I have your attention?" Lara asked.

"What do you think?" he asked, his smile widening. He seized her and rolled her under him.

"Let's forget about everything but just us until you have to go back to court," Lara said to him, reaching up to smooth his hair back from his brow. "Is it a deal?"

"It's a deal," he replied, and kissed her.

Lara made sure that Cal kept his word, diverting all discussion of his legal situation until they eventually had to face it on the day of his final hearing. Neither one of them had much to say as they drove to the courthouse and entered the building, meeting Carol outside the courtroom directly across the hall from the one they had occupied the last time.

"Ready?" Carol said to Cal, who nodded stoically.

"As I'll ever be," he replied.

As soon as they entered Lara noticed that they were not alone. There was a pretty young woman sitting in the front row with an older man in a three-piece suit standing next to her.

"Who's that?" Lara whispered to Carol, as Cal walked ahead of them.

"That's bad news," Carol said grimly. "I was notified yesterday that she had obtained permission to attend the hearing as an interested party, but I decided not to tell Cal. I didn't want him to get worked up about it beforehand."

"But who is it?" Lara asked.

"Maria Winterfield and her lawyer."

Lara looked fearfully at Carol, who nodded grimly. "That's right. Matthew Winterfield's sister. I'm afraid," the lawyer said, "she's here to make sure that the charges against Cal aren't dropped."

Eight

"What can she do?" Lara asked, glancing ahead at Cal to see if he had noticed the extra guests at their little soiree.

Carol shrugged. "The Winterfield name still means something around here, even though the congressman is no longer in office and both Maria and her mother have moved away. To tell you the truth, I was afraid some reporters might get wind of Cal's bail hearing and show up for a story, so I asked the judge to put a press gag order on both proceedings. But somehow these people have a way of finding out what they want to know."

"What people?" Lara asked.

"Rich people," Carol replied flatly, and then looked to the front of the room as the judge entered.

"Where's Canfield?" Lara inquired, scanning the participants for the assistant district attorney.

"He's been replaced," Carol replied, pointing to an older man with graying temples and a clipped moustache. His suit looked expensive and his watch did, too.

"Something tells me his presence is not good news," Lara said dismally.

"Getting bail denied for a former fugitive was expected to be a slam dunk, so a junior ADA like Canfield was thought sufficient to the task," Carol said archly. "When Canfield returned to the DA's office with the surprising news that Cal was free on bail, I imagine there was quite a row. They're not taking a second chance with this."

"So who's that?"

"The District Attorney himself, John Singola."

Cal turned back to look at Lara, and she smiled bravely, masking her concern. She was moving forward to hug him when the judge entered. Carol waved them both into their seats and conversation ceased.

Lara sat in the front row, clasping her trembling hands in her lap. The big guns were out to take Cal back to jail, to take him away from her. Her vision blurred and she felt as if she were slipping out of her seat. She straightened and grasped the sides of her chair, steadying herself as if she were standing on the deck of a rocking ship.

"Are you all right?" Carol asked Lara, bending down to whisper directly into her ear, concern in the lawyer's tone. "You don't look very well."

"I'm scared, Carol."

Carol nodded, then patted Lara's hand before moving up to take her place before the court.

The proceedings began, but as hard as Lara tried to concentrate, the scene continued to swim before her eyes. She tried to fix her gaze on Cal's broad shoulders, but even that landmark failed to provide stability. Her stomach began to churn, and she stood suddenly, bolting from the courtroom as the bailiff intoned the preliminaries of the case.

Lara just made it to ladies' room before losing what little she had eaten for breakfast. Afterward she bathed her face with cold water in the porcelain washbasin, and when she raised her head to look at herself her reflection was ghostly. She leaned against the tiled wall, closing her eyes, and several minutes passed before she heard knocking on the washroom door.

She walked outside unsteadily, to confront the bailiff, who examined her bloodless face with concern.

"Miss, are you all right? Attorney Novak saw you leave and sent me after you," the man said.

Lara nodded. As she did so her vision began to fade again, and the sound of his voice seemed to recede and grow tinny. She reached out helplessly and the bailiff caught her in his arms to prevent her from hitting the floor as she fainted.

Lara woke up in a darkened room. As her eyes adjusted to the gloom she realized that she was in a hospital. It was night outside the window she could see to her left, and when she turned her head the other way she saw Cal asleep in a chair next to her bed.

Gradually the events of the day came back to her, and she sat up suddenly as she remembered the hearing and her abrupt exit from it. What had happened? Why was Cal still free? She called his name, but her voice was so hoarse that the sound came out as a croak.

Lara cleared her throat and tried again. This time her effort resembled his name, and his eyes opened.

"Oh, sweetheart, you're awake!" he said, leaning forward and grasping her hands. "How do you feel?"

"What am I doing here?" she whispered.

"You passed out at the hearing this morning. The bailiff called an ambulance and they brought you here for observation. They wouldn't release you because your vital signs are unstable or some damn thing. Do you remember any of this?"

Lara shook her head.

He lifted one of her hands to his lips. "I've been so worried. I felt so responsible. I'm sure the stress of being in court again brought this on—"

Lara held up her other hand, wetting her dry lips with her tongue, and he quickly poured a glass of water and handed it to her. She took a tentative sip.

"What happened?" she whispered to him, swallowing.

"I just told you, Lara. You passed out—"

She shook her head so violently that he stopped talking.

"At the hearing. The charges..." she muttered.

"Dropped," he replied, grinning hugely.

"Dropped?" she murmured, dazed. "But the DA, Maria Winterfield..."

"Look, Lara, all you have to know now is that it's over. I'm a free man—no more hearings, no more lawyers, no more jail. I'll tell you about it in detail when you're feeling better, but I was supposed to call the nurse if you woke up. That's the only reason they let me stay in here." He stood, reached for the bell cord and pressed the button. When he looked back at Lara he saw that her eyes were swimming with tears.

"Don't cry, baby," he said, bending to kiss her cheek. "You should be happy."

"I am happy," she whispered. "I just can't believe it."

"Neither could I, and for a few minutes there at the beginning I thought I was doomed. But that judge is a stand-up guy. He really gave me a break. Oh, here's your medical team."

A nurse and a doctor bustled in from the corridor. The nurse snapped on the overhead light as the doctor lifted Lara's chart from the holder at the foot of the bed.

"When did she wake up?" the doctor asked Cal. He was a handsome young intern with ink black hair and brows, olive skin and a burly build.

"About five minutes ago."

"Is she talking clearly?"

"Yes."

"Any stuttering or slurring of speech?"

"No."

"Does she seem rational?"

"Perfectly."

"Why don't you ask me?" Lara said irritably. "I'm right here."

"I'm Dr. Marchetti and this is Nurse Langford," the doctor said to Lara, gesturing to his companion.

"Hi," Lara said.

"Could you leave us alone with the patient now, please?" the doctor said to Cal, as the nurse lifted Lara's wrist and then looked at her own watch.

"I'll be right outside in the hall," Cal said to Lara.

Marchetti waited until Cal had left and then said, "You gave that big guy quite a scare today, young lady. I'm working a double shift so I was on duty when you were admitted. I thought I was going to have to book another bed for him when he found out you were here." He lifted Lara's right lid and shone a flashlight into her eye. She winced and blinked.

"How do you feel now?" he asked, pocketing his penlight. The nurse hovered in the background, lowering the window shade.

"Fine, I guess," Lara replied, realizing that it was true.

"Your blood pressure was 98 over 55 when you were admitted," the doctor informed her.

"Is that bad?"

"It isn't good. It's a few blips above a corpse," Marchetti said dryly.

"Oh. Well, you should know that labile blood pressure runs in my family. My grandmother who just died had a lot of trouble stabilizing hers."

"How old was she?"

"Seventy-eight."

He nodded. "You're twenty-seven. Any other ideas?"

Lara shrugged. "I was in a stressful situation. Cal and I were attending his evidentiary hearing and I was very worried."

"Been having any nausea lately?"

"Some."

"Bloating, breast tenderness, swelling of hands or feet?"

Lara stared at him.

He raised his heavily marked brows. "We can't find a thing wrong with you, except that your blood work reveals the presence of human gonadotropin."

"Meaning?"

"That's the hormone secreted by a developing fetus. The home pregnancy tests measure its concentration in the urine."

"You mean..."

He nodded again. "Congratulations. I think I can guess the identity of the father."

Lara looked from him to the nurse in amazement. They were both smiling at her.

"But that can't be..." she murmured.

"Why not?" the doctor said, lifting his wide shoulders. "Judging from the intense devotion displayed by your male companion, it's my strong feeling that your relationship is not platonic. Haven't you missed any periods?"

"I have never been regular, I just thought it was..."

"Stress," the nurse said, and she shot Marchetti a look.

"I'm not stupid," Lara said, as her face grew warm. "I've just been preoccupied..."

"I understand," the doctor said sympathetically.

Cal stuck his head into the room.

"Done yet?" he said.

"Not yet," Marchetti said, and Cal retreated, disappointed.

"Look," the doctor said, "it's none of my business how you handle this piece of information, but you should know that I estimate you are two to three months pregnant. We can run an ultrasound in the morning to establish the age of the fetus and the due date. When you were admitted we didn't administer epenephrine or any other drugs because pregnancy sometimes causes a drop in blood pressure and we didn't want to take any chances. So you don't have to worry about any harm coming to the baby."

Lara nodded, still trying to absorb what he was telling her. A baby!

"So that's that," Dr. Marchetti said briskly. "Your pressure is normal now. You can have something to eat if you want, and you'll be released in the morning. Do you have any questions?"

"Just a request."

"Shoot."

"Don't say anything to Cal about the baby. I want to tell him myself."

"You got it. Nurse Langford, see what this young lady will have from the kitchen, and Miss Daniels,

I'll be back in the morning to check on you. Good night."

Dr. Marchetti swept out the door, and the nurse presented Lara with a check sheet of food items. Lara took the proffered pen and wrote a quick cross next to several selections randomly, handing the nurse the clipboard.

"This will be up shortly. Dinner is over and the kitchen is slow this time of night," the nurse said as she left.

Cal entered immediately. "So? Will you live?"

"Apparently. They're feeding me."

"Good. Can't do enough of that. What's the diagnosis?"

"Blood pressure blues. The curse of the Kellys."

"Who are the Kellys?"

"Rose's people. Kelly was her maiden name."

He nodded. "When do they spring you?"

"Tomorrow. Now tell me about the hearing."

"Nothing doing."

Lara moaned.

"Dr. Marchetti says you need rest, and you're going to get it. We'll have plenty of time to talk in the morning."

"He didn't say I need rest," Lara muttered irritably.

"He said it to me in the hall."

"What else did he tell you?"

"He said that you have very pretty ankles, but I already knew that."

Nurse Langford materialized from the corridor and announced, "I think your guest should be leaving,

Miss Daniels. It's well past visiting hours. The day shift said to let him stay because he was raising such a ruckus, it was either do that or have him arrested."

She cast a sidelong glance at Cal, who grinned back at her charmingly.

"Out," Nurse Langford said to him.

Cal bent to kiss Lara. "I'll be back before you know it," he said, and then looked over his shoulder to wink at her as he left.

"Eat this and then go to sleep," Nurse Langford said, sliding a tray onto the bedside table.

"Thank you," Lara replied, letting her head fall back against her pillow wearily as the soft sounds of the night nurse's padded shoes signaled her departure.

Lara was immediately lost in thought. Cal was free, and she was pregnant. Suddenly the future seemed full of joyful possibilities, but at the same time a new concern had arisen to replace the old ones.

What if Cal didn't want the baby? They had been so preoccupied, first with their stormy relationship and then with Cal's problems, that they had never even discussed having a family. Would the responsibility be too much for him to handle? He had been alone all his life, answerable only to himself, and his past experiences could hardly have given him a positive image of domestic life. Now he would have not only a business to run and a wife to support, but a child to care for as well.

Lara sighed and glanced at the cottage cheese salad and chicken sandwich on her tray. She pushed the table away from the bed and snapped off the light.

Despite having slept most of the day, she was still exhausted, and it would all be waiting for her in the morning.

Lara was awakened at seven for the ultrasound test. She was wheeled through a corridor filled with bustling technicians, then waited in an anteroom for two hours while the technicians walked past her as if she were made of glass. But when she finally saw the image of her baby on the screen, as tiny and embryonic as any illustration in an anatomy book, she started to cry.

Cal's baby was steadily growing inside of her. It was truly a miracle.

Lara was still crying when she was wheeled back into her room and saw Carol Novak waiting for her.

"What are you doing here so early?" Lara asked, as the attorney bent to embrace her.

"You know that head nurse who looks like Mrs. Danvers, the nutty housekeeper in the Hitchcock movie?" Carol asked.

Lara nodded, her head down.

"She went to high school with my older brother and got me past the desk. Hey, hey, what's this? Why the tears?" Carol responded, stepping back as an attendant assisted Lara into a chair and Carol saw her flooded eyes.

Lara waited until the orderly had left with the wheelchair before saying, "I'm pregnant. I just had an ultrasound and saw the baby.'' She wiped her eyes with her fingers and smiled tremulously.

Carol's face went blank with surprise, then she grinned. ''But that's wonderful news!'' Her grin faded slowly. ''Isn't it?'' she said, as an afterthought.

Lara shrugged. ''I'm thrilled about it, Carol, but Cal—well, you know what kind of a life he's had. I just don't know how he's going to take it.''

Carol nodded slowly. ''You think he might not be happy?'' she said sympathetically.

''We weren't planning it. We've spent all of our time since his arrest trying to keep him out of jail. Knitting booties was not exactly high on the agenda. And his own parents abandoned him. Sometimes orphans become bitter and have very negative feelings about family life. 'I did all right without it, who needs it?' That type of thing.''

''And sometimes they go the other way and become determined to have a family of their own and give their children what they never had,'' Carol said. ''I've seen that often enough, too.''

Lara reached for the box of tissues on her tray table and blew her nose. ''It's all too much to deal with at once. The last thing I remember is leaving the hearing room and feeling ill, and now all of a sudden it's over, Cal's free, and I'm pregnant. I feel a little like Dorothy in *The Wizard of Oz.*''

''Not in Kansas anymore?'' Carol said, sitting in the guest chair and setting her briefcase and purse on the floor.

''Definitely not.''

"Did Cal tell you what happened at the hearing?" Carol asked brightly.

"He wouldn't tell me a thing, and I'm bursting with curiosity," Lara replied.

"Well, first Cal went ballistic when he found out you had been taken away in an ambulance and the bailiff had to restrain him," Carol said dryly.

Lara winced. "No wonder Cal didn't want to tell me about it," she said.

"Luckily the judge is an understanding type, and recessed until Cal talked to your doctor and determined that you were okay. The DA was going wild. He wanted a postponement, but Judge Mellon overruled him. And then the judge announced that he had read all of the depositions on file from Cal's arraignment."

"And?'

Carol sighed. "When I was told before the hearing that I wouldn't have to call any witnesses I knew that Judge Mellon's opinion was already formed. The judge was convinced from what he had read that Cal had been unfairly charged, *or* the judge didn't believe a word and didn't want to see the witnesses because having them there in person wouldn't make any difference."

"You never told me that," Lara said sternly.

Carol held up her hand. "There are some things it's better to keep from clients."

"And so?" Lara prompted.

"So Judge Mellon ruled that the coroner's verdict should have been death by misadventure and Cal should not have been charged in the matter. The DA then brought up the assault on the prison guard, and for that offense the judge gave Cal a suspended sentence with a fine and community service."

"What does that mean?"

"You'll have to hang around Hartford for six months while Cal drives for a Hartford emergency squad," Carol answered archly, laughing.

Lara stared. "But what about Maria Winterfield? She was there with her lawyer."

Carol leaned forward conspiratorially. "Well, you're not going to believe this..."

"I don't believe any of it."

"It seems that Maria always thought that Cal's case was, as she put it to me after the hearing, 'a gross miscarriage of justice.' She knew that her brother was a wild kid who'd been spoiled from the cradle upward and, get this, she had been looking for Cal herself for the whole time he was on the run."

"Looking for him?"

"Yes, yes, she had a private detective on the case, who was no more successful in locating your elusive boyfriend than the police were," Carol replied.

"Until my pal Bob Trask gave them a little help," Lara said ruefully.

"Who's Bob Trask? Oh, the cop out in Montana. I saw his name on the arrest reports."

"Right. I was dating him before...before Cal and I became involved. When I dropped Bob, he decided to take out his frustrations by investigating my lover's past."

"And struck the jackpot."

"He certainly thought so. But why was Maria Winterfield tracking Cal?"

"It seems she had attended Cal's arraignment and was as disgusted by the outcome as I was when I read the transcript. She knew her father had bought everybody off—it had been his approach to solving problems all his life. When she heard Cal had escaped, even though she had to go back to Europe she hired a detective to locate Cal and try to rectify the situation."

"How did she know about his hearing yesterday?"

"The private detective she hired has a friend on the local police force. The detective called Maria about the bail hearing, but when she couldn't make that, she decided she would get here for the hearing on Cal's charges."

"And I thought she was in the courtroom to make sure Cal stayed in jail," Lara said in a wondering tone.

"So did I. It seems she wrote a letter to Judge Mellon expressing her feelings on the subject of Cal's arrest, and that, together with the depositions, convinced the judge to let Cal go."

"I should thank her," Lara murmured.

"I already did," Carol said, rising from her chair. "She was on a plane back to Italy last night. You can write to her if you like. I have the address."

"You're leaving?" Lara asked.

"I have an appointment in my office in fifteen minutes," Carol said, looking at her watch.

"I don't know how to thank you for everything

you've done for Cal and me,'' Lara said quietly, aware of the inadequacy of the simple statement.

''You'll get my bill,'' Carol said, smiling. She bent to kiss Lara's cheek and added, ''Take care of that baby, and keep in touch.''

''I will.'' Lara watched Carol walk briskly out the door, then started to cry again.

She had expected to feel some strong emotions when or if Cal was released, but a pressing desire to bawl like an infant was not one of them. The constant weepiness must be due to the pregnancy, or else she had been more on edge than she realized and the crying was just an expression of overwhelming relief.

Dr. Marchetti breezed in, took her blood pressure, announced that she was ten weeks pregnant and said that he was processing her release papers. He also gave her the name of a local OB-GYN, a still shot from her ultrasound film and a prescription for prenatal vitamins. Lara was studying the picture, which showed shadowy eyes and the clear outline of one tiny hand, when Cal arrived.

She shoved the film under her pillow, pretending that she was adjusting the blanket on her bed.

Cal was wearing blue jeans and a pale blue shirt that set off his dark good looks to perfection. He looked rested, relaxed, as if a weight had been lifted from his shoulders, as indeed it had.

Was Lara about to replace it with another one?

He handed her a bouquet of white roses, her favorite, as he bent to kiss her.

''Hello, gorgeous,'' he said.

''Hi, darling.''

"Well, get ready, I'm now prepared to tell you all about what you missed at the hearing," he said, with his most engaging smile.

"Too late. Carol was here earlier and she filled me in, right down to the letter to the judge from Maria Winterfield."

His smile faded. "Damn. I was going to act it all out for you, too. Complete with an improvised, dramatic conclusion during which Carol elopes with Judge Mellon."

"Spare me. Could you put these in water? There's a jug right over there."

Cal got the plastic jug and filled it in the bathroom, then returned to place the makeshift vase on Lara's table. He sat opposite her and folded his arms.

"So if you got the rundown from Carol, I guess we have nothing to say to each other," he informed her mischievously.

"I have something to say to you," Lara replied quietly.

Her tone alerted him to her state of mind, and he looked at her sharply. "Baby, what is it?" he said, leaning forward to grasp her hands. "Is something wrong?"

"I hope not," she whispered.

He waited, searching her face.

"I think this may..." She stopped, biting her lip.

His grip tightened. "Lara, look what we've been through together. We're home free now. You can tell me anything."

She took him at his word.

"I'm pregnant," she blurted.

She would never forget how his face was transformed by the news. First it registered nothing, as he absorbed her statement, then it was suddenly suffused with feeling. He raised her hands to his lips and closed his eyes.

"Cal?" she said softly.

His eyes opened. "I love you," he whispered.

"Does that mean it's okay?" Lara asked shakily.

He knelt in front of her chair and put his head in her lap, wrapping his arms around her waist. Lara stroked his hair and began to cry again, quietly.

"Say something," Lara finally told him through her tears.

He shook his head, unable to look up at her.

"Cal, please talk to me."

He lifted his head and gazed at her, a haunted expression she had never seen before in his eyes.

"I've always wanted a family," he murmured.

"Really?" Lara replied. "I know you said that you wanted one as a kid, but what about now? You're not just saying you do because one is already on the way?"

"No, sweetheart. Oh, no. How could you even think that, Lara?"

"I don't know, Cal. This news was so unexpected I wasn't sure what to think. I was so afraid that after all of your recent trouble you wouldn't be able to handle the responsibility."

"I want what I never had," he said simply. "But what could I offer anybody? Especially after the arrest, when I was on the run, the prospect seemed hopeless. And then when I met you, it was even worse, because you were everything I had dreamed of for so long. I couldn't have you or the house and the kids, any of it."

"You can have it now," Lara said, and got out of her chair to retrieve the ultrasound photo.

"What's this?" he said, taking it from her hand.

"Your baby. I had a test this morning and the technician took a picture of the child."

Cal stared down at the sheet of plastic, his lips curving upward, his eyes full of wonder. "Is that a hand?" he asked.

"Yes."

"So small," he murmured. "Is it a boy or a girl?"

"It's too soon to tell. Do you care?"

He shook his head, transfixed by the image of his child developing in Lara's womb.

An orderly appeared in the doorway and said, "I've got your release papers right here, Miss Daniels. I'll bring you a wheelchair and then you can sign them. We're releasing you."

"Did you hear that, Cal?" Lara said.

"Hmm?" he said, still staring at the picture.

"The hospital is releasing me."

He looked up. "About time." He put the picture into his pocket, then took her hands again and raised her, pulling her into his arms.

"It's you and me from now on," he said huskily. "And junior, too, of course. Nothing's going to stop us now."

Lara put her head on his shoulder and closed her eyes, her happiness complete.

Epilogue

Lara brushed her hair vigorously, bending forward from the waist and stroking upward from the roots. She was just about to straighten when she felt a kiss on the back of her neck.

"Who is it?" she said.

"Guess," came the reply.

"The man of my dreams?"

"Right the first time." Cal took the brush from her hand and turned her around to face him, pushing the loose strands of hair back from her forehead.

"Is Rose asleep?" he asked.

"Finally," Lara sighed. "We had to put Bert and Ernie, Barney and Baby Bop, three dolls and a yellow giraffe to bed first, but we are at last in dreamland."

"And you're still sane," Cal said.

"Don't count on it," Lara replied, rolling her eyes dramatically, and he laughed. "I have never seen any human being resist sleep the way that child does."

"That's what it's like to be two," Cal answered, tossing his wallet and keys on the dresser.

"Come with me." Lara took her husband's hand and led him out of the bedroom, down the hall to the kitchen.

"Where are we going?" he asked. "I kind of had plans in mind for the bed."

"I have something to show you."

"You can show me what's under that transparent gown you're wearing. I'm a lot more interested in that than whatever you have in the kitchen."

"Patience, please."

They stopped before the table, which displayed a silver bucket of ice containing a bottle of champagne.

"Very nice. What's it for?"

"We're celebrating."

"I'll bite. What are we celebrating?" Cal asked.

"Take a stab at it."

"Did Holstrom agree to sell us that Arabian horse?" he said.

"Better than that."

"Every other stud farm in Montana went bust and we have a monopoly?"

Lara stepped forward and kissed him lightly on the lips.

"I'm pregnant again," she announced.

A slow smile spread over his face. "Really?"

She smiled back at him. "Really. I saw Dr. Perry

while you were in Sadler today. He says I'm ten weeks along."

Cal put his arms around her and drew her close. "Rose Marie is going to have competition," he said.

"She'll go on strike," Lara replied.

He laughed. "She'll get used to it. They all do. So I guess the champagne is only for me, huh?"

"That's right. I just thought it was a nice idea," Lara whispered, relaxing against his shoulder as they both looked out the picture window over the moonlit grass.

"You've seen too many movies," Cal said teasingly.

"Yes, I know. I'm stuck in a celluloid dream, a sucker for happily ever after."

"We're living it," Cal said into her ear.

Lara nodded silently.

"Rose would be very happy," he added quietly.

"Do you think so?" Lara replied, her eyes filling.

"Of course. She wanted us to be together, and now we're living in her house, running her business, having her great-grandchildren. The first one is even named after her. She would be thrilled."

"But she didn't live to see it," Lara said sadly, wiping her eyes with the back of her hand.

Cal hugged her tighter. "She knows," he said.

"Do you believe that?"

"Yes, I do. I believe in everything since I met you. Nothing is impossible." He reached over her shoulder and began untying the neck of his wife's nightgown.

"What are you doing?" she asked.

"Undressing you. Any objections?"

"None," Lara said, hooking her arms around his neck as her gown slid to the floor in a silken puddle.

"Mmm," Cal said, running his hands down Lara's back luxuriously and closing his eyes. "You feel so good. I've been looking forward to this all day."

"While you were taking that foal to the vet in Sadler?" Lara asked mischievously.

"All the way there and back," he admitted, grinning as he picked her up and carried her in to their bed.

"Your body is so beautiful," he said, dropping down next to her. He ran his forefinger from the base of her throat down to the valley between her breasts.

"Enjoy it while it lasts," Lara said dryly. "In six months I'll look like a blimp."

"You'll be beautiful then, too. You were with Rose." He placed his palm on her bare belly.

Lara covered his hand with hers. "Does it make up for the past, Cal?" she asked. "What we have today, does it make up for everything bad that happened to you?"

He embraced her and kissed her. "Yes," he said.

"Are you sure?"

"I'm sure. The past makes me appreciate the present more," he said against her mouth.

And then the talking stopped.

* * * * *

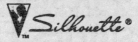

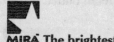

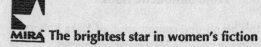

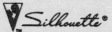

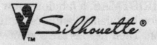